Panic

by

Joseph Goodrich

SAMUEL FRENCH

FOUNDED 1830

NEW YORK HOLLYWOOD LONDON TORONTO

SAMUELFRENCH.COM

ISBN 978-0-573-66277-5   Printed in U.S.A.   #19090

IMPORTANT BILLING AND CREDIT REQUIREMENTS

All producers of *PANIC must* give credit to the Author of the Play in all programs distributed in connection with performances of the Play, and in all instances in which the title of the Play appears for the purposes of advertising, publicizing or otherwise exploiting the Play and/or a production. The name of the Author *must* appear on a separate line on which no other name appears, immediately following the title and *must* appear in size of type not less than fifty percent of the size of the title type.

"Panic" received the 2008 Edgar Allen Poe Award for Best Play from the Mystery Writers of America. "Panic" premiered in the International Mystery Writers' Festival at RiverPark Center Owensboro, KY. Zev Buffman, Festival co-chair and president and CEO of RiverPark Center

CHARACTERS

HENRY LOCKWOOD
ALAIN DUPLAY
EMMA LOCKWOOD
MIRIAM STOCKTON
LILIANE BERNARD
JULIET COTTARD

PLACE

A large, ornately furnished hotel room.
Paris, 1963.

TIME

Act one, *scene one*: early one evening.
Scene two: several hours later
Scene three: next afternoon
Scene four: that evening

Act two, *scene one*: the same
Scene two: early next morning.
Scene three: two days later, mid-morning.

ACT I

1.

(Darkness.

Lights up.

HENRY LOCKWOOD – *a large man in his early 60s –*
and **ALAIN DUPLAY** – *dark, compact, early 30s – on*
either side of a large table.

Both are in formal evening wear.

A large microphone, attached to a Revox reel-to-reel
recorder, is positioned between them.)

LOCKWOOD. The young man is alone in Paris. He doesn't
speak the language. He's running out of money.
There's no one to help him, no one he can ask for
help. The concierge at his small, dingy hotel is giving
him an increasingly fishy eye, and he knows he's one
small step from sleeping under a bridge by the Seine.
Hunger gnaws at his body. Regret consumes his heart.
The beauty of the city around him tears at his soul.
He has nowhere to go. Nowhere but down. As if he
could fall any lower…There must be a way to put an
end to this situation. To end this pain. And there is.
(Pause.) One night – when sleep is impossible and
every thought is torture –

(He picks up a letter opener.)

– he sees…with achingly clarity…a means of escape.
(Pause.) His only question is: wrist or throat?…Wrist
– or throat? *(Pause.)* The hours pass. Sunlight filters
through the blind. Voices are heard in street. It's morning. A midsummer morning in Paris…Perhaps today
the unexpected letter? The fortuitous encounter?

5

Perhaps today…unimaginable as it seems in his tiny room in the Rue de Nesle…Love? *(Pause.)*

(He places the letter opener on the table.)

…Perhaps. *(Pause.)* What does he do next? *(Pause.)* What would you do? *(Pause.)*

DUPLAY. He…leaves his room. He goes into the street. He walks.

LOCKWOOD. Exactly. And we follow him as he walks. We see him asking strangers for money. A rich woman humiliates him in front of a crowd, then holds out a 100-Franc note. He refuses it. It's true he has nothing, but he hasn't lost his pride. He may be young and foolish –

DUPLAY. And hungry –

LOCKWOOD. And hungry…But he still has his dignity. That can't be bought – and the crowd knows it. The fat butcher in a blue smock says something and the crowd laughs. A taxi driver says something else. Soon the entire crowd is jeering and jibing at the rich woman. She has her dignity, as well – rather too much of it, actually – and she calls to a passing *gendarme*, who approaches. 'What is the trouble, Madame?' 'This young man,' she says, pointing a lacquered nail at the boy, 'this young man tried to rob me.' A frozen moment as the boy weighs the odds and the crowd watches. – Then action, and noise: The boy runs. The gendarme blows his whistle and gives chase. The boy melts into the crowd and dashes into the dark, narrow back streets. The *gendarme* follows in hot pursuit. The boy turns one way – police. He hurries down an alleyway, turns the corner – more police. He opens a door and enters. He follows a dimly-lit passage through a building, emerges into the sunshine of a courtyard, runs under the archway leading to the street…and smack into a funeral procession. He joins the throng and shuffles slowly along through the streets, surrounded by mourners. The gendarmes search the crowd in vain. The boy moves with the mourners into the cemetery. He drifts away as soon as he can. He sits on a bench in an isolated corner of the cemetery. He catches his breath.

DUPLAY. A narrow escape.

LOCKWOOD. Indeed. He searches his pockets, finds a crumpled cigarette, sits back in the sun and smokes. The barrel of a gun enters the frame...

DUPLAY. Yes?

LOCKWOOD. He looks up. He sees the gun barrel. He smiles.

DUPLAY. – He smiles?

LOCKWOOD. Yes. He smiles. He raises his arms in the air. We cut to another angle: a little boy in a cowboy hat and short pants, holding a cap gun on our hero. The little boy scowls. He pulls the trigger. Our hero cries out, falls off the bench, sprawls in the dirt. He lies there. The little boy approaches. 'I didn't kill you,' says the boy. 'I just wounded you. It was the other man I killed.' 'What man?' 'The man over there. I shot him and he fell down and he's dead.' Our hero sits up. 'Where is he?' The little boy begins to speak, but a large, heavily-rouged woman in a floral-print sun dress and large picture hat comes around the corner. 'Jerome,' she says, 'Come along now.' She turns to our hero. 'I hope Jerome hasn't been bothering you.' 'He says he's killed someone,' says our hero. The woman's red lips curl in a fulsome smile. 'Jerome has shot 27 Indians and five French policemen today, and that's just this morning.' She steers the little boy off at a trot down the path to the cemetery gates. Our hero starts off in the same direction as Jerome and his rather vibrant mother. As he's passing a particular cluster of tombstones, he hears – very soft, very low – someone moaning. His pace quickens. We cut from a medium-close moving shot of his face to a point-of-view shot of the changing perspective of tombstones, back and forth – until we see the man...

DUPLAY. The man...

LOCKWOOD. A well-dressed older man lying between two large tombstones. Our hero cuts through the graves and helps the man to his feet. He hasn't been shot – to Jerome's sorrow, no doubt, if the boy had been allowed to linger – but collapsed from the heat. Our hero helps the man out of the cemetery and to a seat at a nearby café. *(Pause.)*

DUPLAY. And?

LOCKWOOD. And what?

DUPLAY. What happens next?

(**EMMA LOCKWOOD** *– early 60s, cane in one hand, book in another – enters.*)

EMMA. Henry?

(**LOCKWOOD** *and* **DUPLAY** *rise.*)

LOCKWOOD. Emma.

DUPLAY. Good evening, Madame Lockwood.

EMMA. Am I interrupting?

LOCKWOOD. Not at all. We were just winding up for the day. Stop the tape, Alain.

DUPLAY. But what happens next?

LOCKWOOD. He's invited to the man's house, solves the mystery of the man's murder and blackmails the guilty party – the lovely but haughty daughter. He lives a comfortably discreet existence until he meets an unexpectedly violent end engineered by the daughter's lover...The man to whom the entire story has been related over drinks.

(**DUPLAY** *leans toward the mike.*)

DUPLAY. This is the end of day three of my interview with Monsieur Lockwood for the *Carnet Du Cinema*, 17th August, 1963.

(He hits the recorder's 'stop' button.)

Alors – c'est tout. Thank you for waiting, Madame.

EMMA. I just came out to see if you were still here.

LOCKWOOD. Oh, yes. We won't be going for a while yet.

EMMA. Have you checked with Antoine about a taxi?

LOCKWOOD. Alain has arranged for a limousine.

EMMA. *Merci*, Alain.

DUPLAY. *C'est un plaisir*, Madame. Only the best will do for Monsieur Lockwood.

LOCKWOOD. You didn't think I'd leave without saying good-bye?

EMMA. I didn't *think* so, no.

DUPLAY. Madame Lockwood, you are a gift from the angels.

EMMA. That's sweet of you, Alain. Now give me a kiss and make us a drink, would you?

DUPLAY. A privilege, Madame Lockwood.

(*He moves to kiss her cheek.*

EMMA *moves, too, and* **DUPLAY'S** *lips briefly meet hers.*)

EMMA. – Now help me to the couch.

(**DUPLAY** *does, then crosses to the drinks table.*)

How's the interview going? Have you given away all your secrets?

LOCKWOOD. I'm keeping a few of them for myself. How are you feeling?

EMMA. Fine, I suppose. I've been resting. Just as the doctor ordered.

LOCKWOOD. Have you had your medicine?

EMMA. No. I'll have Miriam give it to me when she gets back.

LOCKWOOD. You see how easy it is? You rest, you take your medicine...

EMMA. It's boring as hell, to tell the truth, but I do it because I have to.

LOCKWOOD. Emma, if you want to get better...

EMMA. I know, I know...

DUPLAY. The heart is a delicate instrument, Madame Lockwood. It must be treated with care. I know this for a fact.

EMMA. Really?

DUPLAY. As a child, Madame Lockwood, I myself suffer from the...*palpitations.*

EMMA. A healthy young man like you?

DUPLAY. I swear it, Madame.

EMMA. But you're fine now?

DUPLAY. Madame, could a sick man do this?

(*He stands on his hands, 'walks' a few paces, then returns to his feet with a flourish.*)

DUPLAY. *Et voila!*

(**EMMA** *applauds.*)

EMMA. *Encore! Encore!*

LOCKWOOD. You've got something to aim for now, Emma.

EMMA. I don't think I'll be trying *that.*

LOCKWOOD. Oh, but I can see you now – merrily strolling down the Champs Elysees, feet in the air...

EMMA. I'd rather do that than lie in bed reading all day. I'm so tired of doing nothing, Henry...Did I tell you I finished Patty's new book?

(**DUPLAY**, *drinks in hand, crosses to* **EMMA.**)

LOCKWOOD. What'd you think?

EMMA. Patty...is morbid.

LOCKWOOD. Indeed she is.

DUPLAY. Madame Lockwood, *votre boisson.*

EMMA. Thank you, Alain.

(**DUPLAY** *crosses to* **LOCKWOOD.**)

LOCKWOOD. Has the new one got any potential?

EMMA. I think so.

DUPLAY. Monsieur Lockwood.

LOCKWOOD. Thank you.

(**DUPLAY** *crosses back to the drinks table, takes his drink, and crosses to the sofa.*)

Is it anything for us?

EMMA. Absolutely. You'd have to cut out the homoerotic elements, change the main character and re-work the third act, but apart from that...

LOCKWOOD. I like a challenge.

EMMA. I know you do.

(She sips her drink.)

Soda water!

LOCKWOOD. If you want to get better...

EMMA. I know. God, how I know! But a bit of scotch now and then wouldn't constitute a crime, would it?

LOCKWOOD. Emma...

EMMA. All right, all right...But I can't see the point of getting better if I'm not allowed to have any fun at all.

LOCKWOOD. You were saying about the book?

EMMA. The book, yes...It's kind of a mess in some ways, but something about it hooks me.

LOCKWOOD. What's the story?

EMMA. It's set in Florence. An American writer becomes obsessed with a young Italian girl, who's beautiful beyond belief – olive skin, masses of dark hair. She's *ripe*. But she's also sullen and promiscuous...A lovely and dangerous animal.

LOCKWOOD. I like that...He shouldn't be a writer, though.

EMMA. I was thinking he could be an architect. Something visual.

LOCKWOOD. Possibly.

EMMA. What's wrong with his being an architect?

LOCKWOOD. He could be a painter. That's even more visual.

EMMA. Well, one day he goes into a shop and sees a watch there for sale. It's his watch, a gift from his father. He thought he'd lost it. The shopkeeper tells him the girl brought it in and sold it to him. The American buys it back, finds the girl in the *trattoria* where she works, and they have a violent argument. It turns out she's only been using him for what she can get – the flowers, the gifts, the attention – and robbing him blind. And the whole town knows it. He's a joke, a fool. He walks out of the *trattoria* as they all laugh at him…Two days later her bruised and naked body is dragged out of the Arno. She's been raped and her skull's been caved in like a rotten watermelon. All that soft, lucious skin, those long raven tresses – just a decaying lump of battered, bloated flesh…We'd have to change that. Soften it some.

DUPLAY. *Pour quoi*, Madame?

EMMA. What?

DUPLAY. Why must you change the book?

EMMA. We want the movie to be made, that's why.

LOCKWOOD. One can only get so much past the censors. Even today. Though God knows I try.

EMMA. And God knows the studio objects to the stuff you try to slip past them.

LOCKWOOD. Audiences don't.

EMMA. Not usually. But remember what happened with *Infamous?*

LOCKWOOD. That had nothing to do with the script.

EMMA. It had a great deal to do with the audience, though. – Mr. Lockwood had made this marvelous movie, it had just opened, and then what happened? Ingrid ran off with Roberto.

DUPLAY. It is a superb film.

EMMA. Yes, it is – and I'm sure all three people who saw it will agree with you.

LOCKWOOD. That was over ten years ago, Emma. Times have changed. Ingrid's got her second Oscar now. I think it's safe to say she's been forgiven.

EMMA. Times haven't changed at all, Henry. Just read the newspapers. One mistake, one unfortunate slip…and they'll feed you to the lions. The merest *hint* of scandal is all it takes.

LOCKWOOD. Nonsense.

DUPLAY. I believe you are right, Madame. Americans love the *idea* of sin, but only the idea.

EMMA. It's a strange country, Alain. They'll give you the key to the city in the morning, then crucify you at lunch. And for what? Loving the wrong person. Holding unfashionable beliefs. So much talk about being free, and so little actual freedom…It's a shame.

LOCKWOOD. Emma, if you keep this up, Alain will think you don't like America.

EMMA. That couldn't be further from the truth. I love America. It's been very good to us. We've been lucky… Very lucky.

DUPLAY. I spoke with the Barzmans about this only the other day. They have not had such luck.

EMMA. You saw them? How are they? How's Ben doing?

DUPLAY. Not well.

EMMA. Same thing as before?

DUPLAY. His heart, yes. *(Pause.)* So – you will change the book?

EMMA. Not all of it. We'll keep the basic situation: an American involved with an Italian girl who gets murdered, and the search for the killer.

LOCKWOOD. What's wrong with the third act?

EMMA. Well, the American's guilty, for one thing.

LOCKWOOD. The painter?

EMMA. You mean the architect?

LOCKWOOD. You say he's guilty?

EMMA. Yes. We've been lead to believe it was someone else, but it was the American all along.

LOCKWOOD. Cary would never go for that.

EMMA. He's too old for the part, isn't he?

LOCKWOOD. Don't let him hear you say that.

EMMA. It's the truth. He *is* too old.

LOCKWOOD. Not if we tailor it for him.

EMMA. Reading the book, I was picturing Jimmy. He's so good at being obsessed. And he really *is* an American. He's the perfect fish-out-of-water. And I'll tell you this: Cary will never play a homosexual – latent or otherwise.

LOCKWOOD. And you think Jimmy will?

EMMA. He's not as worried about his reputation as Cary.

LOCKWOOD. The day Jimmy agrees to play a homosexual is the day I drop dead from shock.

EMMA. That's why we have to change it.

LOCKWOOD. Is it terribly overt?

EMMA. Not terribly, no, but it *is* Patty's book. You don't have to look too closely, if you know what I mean…It's the American's relationship with the brother, mostly.

LOCKWOOD. The brother of the Italian girl?

EMMA. Yes. He enters the scene when the police investigation stalls. He becomes rather – infatuated with the American. There's a scene, for instance, where they've been out swimming together. The brother admires the American's clothes. May he try them on? Of course – if the American may try on the brother's clothes. Fair is fair, after all. So they dress up as each other and then go to a tavern where they pretend to *be* each other. They walk back to the American's house, arm in arm, drunk as coots…The American can't help but notice how strongly the brother resembles the sister, how handsome – how attractive, really – the brother is. Why, he could almost be his sister. The same dark hair, the same olive skin, the same insanely kissable lips…The brother stumbles, the American puts an arm around him…And so on. You can see the problem with all *that*.

LOCKWOOD. It sounds delightful.

EMMA. Henry…

LOCKWOOD. I should like to see how much of that I could smuggle in. Give them something to talk about in Indianapolis. Some Italian actor buzzing around Jimmy's speedway...

EMMA. You're not serious, are you?

LOCKWOOD. Let's see what we can get away with. Why not?

EMMA. Mr. Lockwood and I have this discussion every time he makes a movie. I urge caution, and he throws it to the winds. What am I going to do with him, Alain?

LOCKWOOD. She takes this awfully seriously, doesn't she?

EMMA. You're one to point fingers.

LOCKWOOD. What she doesn't realize, Alain, is something very simple: it's only a movie. But just listen to her.

EMMA. 'Only a movie,' he says. You know that's not true, Henry. It's meat and drink for you. No – it's more than that. It's *breathing.* 'Only a movie,' indeed.

LOCKWOOD. Carrying on like this in front of Alain...

EMMA. Alain doesn't mind – do you, Alain?

DUPLAY. Not at all.

LOCKWOOD. Mrs. Lockwood is convinced she's an expert in these matters. I've spent almost 40 years trying to disabuse her of that notion. Without any success whatsoever.

EMMA. But he's enjoyed every moment of it.

LOCKWOOD. That I have. *(Pause.)* Is this something that Whit could work on?

EMMA. Whit would be perfect...If, of course, you really think it's worth the bother.

LOCKWOOD. What do you think?

EMMA. If you like the ending, I'd say yes.

LOCKWOOD. What happens?

EMMA. The American stages his own death, assumes the brother's identity and escapes to Rome when the police get too close to the truth. They track him to the Coliseum and pursue him through the moon-lit ruins. Shadows on stone...Pools of darkness...A desperate man running through the void...

LOCKWOOD. Have Miriam call Harper's first thing in the morning and see if the rights are available.

EMMA. She called them this afternoon.

(*A clock chimes the half-hour: 6:30.*)

Shouldn't you be going?

DUPLAY. Madame Lockwood is right. It would be wise to leave now.

LOCKWOOD. I suppose so.

EMMA. Let me see your tie.

(**LOCKWOOD** *crosses to* **EMMA**, *who adjust his tie.*)

…Nervous?

LOCKWOOD. Petrified.

EMMA. They'll never know it…There.

LOCKWOOD. Do you think we have time for another drink?

DUPLAY. I do not think so, no.

LOCKWOOD. Well, this one did the trick, I must say. If you should fail as a filmmaker, you've got a sterling career ahead of you as a bartender.

EMMA. You're making a movie?

DUPLAY. Yes, Madame. I hope so.

EMMA. That's wonderful.

DUPLAY. We are still working out the financial aspects, but the script is done, I have the actors in mind…If the money is not a problem, we make the film.

EMMA. Why should it be?

DUPLAY. I am not…liked, Madame. In my articles I have said many things against the French producers of film, and they are not disposed to assist me. I must even wear a disguise to go to Cannes. They have guards there with my picture to keep me out. They hate me. They have closed their ranks against me. They wish for my downfall…I love it.

LOCKWOOD. But you've found someone who'll take the risk?

DUPLAY. As I say, the deal is not yet done, but I have my hopes.

LOCKWOOD. The only thing more difficult than making a movie is finding the money to make a movie…Except making a movie.

DUPLAY. They can try to stop me. They will not succeed. No matter what they do, they will not stop me. They all say I live in a dream, and I tell them, 'Yes – and that dream is called the cinema.'

EMMA. I like this young man, Henry. He's got spirit. – You'll make your movie no matter what and show them all, eh?

DUPLAY. Madame – I shall annihilate them.

(**MIRIAM STOCKTON** – *business outfit, hat and gloves – enters with packages and papers.*)

EMMA. Bravo for you.

MIRIAM. Good evening, all.

LOCKWOOD. Miriam.

DUPLAY. Madame Stockton.

EMMA. Hello, Miriam.

(*Miriam crosses to a table, sets the packages down.*)

MIRIAM. I didn't think you'd be here, Mr. Lockwood. Isn't the screening at seven?

LOCKWOOD. We're just on our way out.

MIRIAM. Well, I'm glad I caught you. You'll want to see these.

(*She crosses to* **LOCKWOOD**.)

More telegrams.

(*She hands* **LOCKWOOD** *a telegram.*)

Billy Wilder.

(*She hands him another.*)

George Cukor.

(*She hands him another.*)

Howard Hawks.

(She hands him another.)

And Jerry Wasserstein.

DUPLAY. …Jerry Wasserstein?

LOCKWOOD. My agent.

MIRIAM. They all wish you the best. – Oh, Mrs. Lockwood. I stopped by Galignani's and got the books you wanted. Should I put them in your room?

EMMA. That's not necessary, dear. I'll take them in later myself.

MIRIAM. And I stopped by the gallery and got the picture. And then I picked up that dish for Melinda – which I'll send off tomorrow – and the scarf for Miss Kahn – which I'll also send tomorrow – and then because I was hot and my feet were tired I stopped at Berthillon's for a *crème glacee*. And then –

LOCKWOOD. Emma, listen to what Billy wrote: 'Dear Hank: Here's to a huge success. Appendix removed yesterday, so I had a grand opening myself. Love to Emma.'

EMMA. Darling Billy.

MIRIAM. How thoughtful.

DUPLAY. I don't care for his films, but that is very nice, I think. *(Pause.)*

LOCKWOOD. You don't like Billy Wilder's films?

DUPLAY. I do not.

LOCKWOOD. *Double Indemnity. Lost Weekend. Sunset Boulevard. Witness For The Prosecution.* You find none of those worthy of your admiration and respect?

*(**DUPLAY** opens and closes the fingers of a hand.)*

DUPLAY. Blop-blop-blop-blop-blop. All they do is talk. Film is not about talk. It is about movement.

LOCKWOOD. …You're sure about that?

DUPLAY. Yes.

LOCKWOOD. Mr. Wilder's movies don't have enough movement, is that what you're saying?

DUPLAY. Well...

LOCKWOOD. And his characters talk too much?

DUPLAY. That is my opinion, yes. *(Pause.)*

LOCKWOOD. Well, you happen to be wrong. *(Pause.)*

(He crosses to **EMMA** *and* **MIRIAM.***)*

LOCKWOOD. Keep an eye on Mrs. Lockwood, Miriam.

MIRIAM. Yes, Mr. Lockwood.

EMMA. Henry, I'm not five years old!

LOCKWOOD. You're my dove. That's what you are. My beautiful dove.

(He kisses **EMMA.***)*

I'll call to let you know how it went.

EMMA. This is the first time ever I haven't been with you. And I'm not happy about it.

LOCKWOOD. Neither am I.

EMMA. I was looking forward so much to being with you tonight.

LOCKWOOD. You're always with me, Emma. Always.

(He kisses her again.)

...Well, Alain? Shall we?

(He starts for the door, stops when **DUPLAY** *doesn't follow.*

Alain?

DUPLAY. Monsieur Lockwood, I mean nothing against Monsieur Wilder. All I mean to say is that if – as I believe – movement is the essence of – the very heart of – film, no one's films *move* more grandly, more beautifully, more poetically than yours. If it is a crime to prefer your films to Monsieur Wilder's, then I am guilty, and I gladly proclaim my crime to the world. That is all I mean and I apologize if I offended you.

LOCKWOOD. My dear boy, I've been working in Hollywood for almost 30 years. *Nothing* offends me. But you really should give Billy another chance.

(DUPLAY crosses toward the door.)

LOCKWOOD. I won't be gone long, mother.

EMMA. God bless.

MIRIAM. Good night, Mr. Lockwood.

LOCKWOOD. Miriam.

DUPLAY. *Bon soir, Mesdames.*

(LOCKWOOD exits, followed by DUPLAY.)

LOCKWOOD *(off)* You really prefer my films to Billy's?

DUPLAY. *(off)* Monsieur Lockwood – I tell you –

(Sound of door opening and closing. Pause.)

MIRIAM. Well...

(She crosses to the packages, picks one up, unties it.

DUPLAY enters.)

DUPLAY. I beg your pardon. I forgot my cigarettes.

(He picks them up, pockets them.)

A bientot, Mesdames.

EMMA. Goodnight, Alain.

MIRIAM. Good night.

(He exits.

MIRIAM picks up a stack of books.)

I'll put these on your nightstand.

(She exits.

EMMA rises, moves slowly to the balcony.

MIRIAM – small bottle in hand – enters.)

MIRIAM. Time for your medicine, Mrs. Lockwood.

EMMA. Could you mix it with a bit of scotch this time?

MIRIAM. I don't think so, Mrs. Lockwood.

(MIRIAM crosses to the drinks table, sets the bottle down.

She pours Evian water into a glass.)

EMMA. I suppose you're right, damn it all...You *are* right. I've got to stay alive.

(**MIRIAM** *removes the medicine bottle's cap, squeezes drops into the glass, stirs the mixture.*)

I have to. Where would Mr. Lockwood be without me?

(**MIRIAM**, *with glass, crosses to the balcony.*)

MIRIAM. Lost, Mrs. Lockwood, that's where he'd be.

EMMA. …There they go.

(*They watch. Pause.*

MIRIAM *holds out the glass.*)

MIRIAM. Here you are.

(**EMMA** *takes the glass.*)

EMMA. Thank you.

(*She takes a sip, grimaces, imitates W.C. Fields.*)

'Once, for a period of several days, I was forced to subsist on nothing but bread and water.'

(*She drinks the rest quickly, hands the glass to* **MIRIAM**.

MIRIAM *crosses to the drinks table, sets the glass down.*)

MIRIAM. I think I'll do a bit of work, Mrs. Lockwood, if that's all right.

EMMA. Go right ahead.

MIRIAM. And wouldn't it be a good idea if you were to –

EMMA. Get some rest?…Yes, yes, yes. But let me enjoy a little of this lovely evening…

MIRIAM. Yes, Mrs. Lockwood.

(**MIRIAM** *crosses to the desk.*

She sits, opens a notebook, uncaps a fountain pen.)

EMMA. …I don't think she knows where she's going.

MIRIAM. Mrs. Lockwood?

EMMA. That woman in the street. First she goes one way, then the other, up and down the pavement.

MIRIAM. Really?

EMMA. Oh, yes…

(**MIRIAM** *flips through the notebook, sets it aside.*

She opens another, flips through it, writes...)

...Now she's stopped.

MIRIAM. What, Mrs. Lockwood?

EMMA. That woman in the street. A scrawny little thing in a red coat...She's crossing the street now...

MIRIAM. You really should go get some rest, Mrs. Lockwood.

EMMA. I will. I will...

MIRIAM. You know you've got your appointment with the doctor tomorrow, and –

EMMA. She's pointing at me.

MIRIAM. What, Mrs. Lockwood?

EMMA. ...I think she's pointing at me. That girl in the red coat...Yes, she is. She's pointing at me.

MIRIAM. How odd.

(*She flips a few pages forward in the notebook.*

She hits 'rewind'.)

EMMA. ...Now she's walking away...What a lovely evening for a walk...Oh, what a lovely evening...

(**MIRIAM** *hits the 'play' button.*

Lights fade.)

2.

(Darkness.)

LOCKWOOD'S VOICE. A movie, you see, is like a clock. One assembles it with care, winds it up, sets the alarm – then forgets about it. But the audience *knows* the alarm has been set…And that it will go off. But they don't – know – when…*That* is how you create suspense.

(Lights up.

MIRIAM, *alone, at desk.)*

You see, Alain, a director is first of all a craftsman, a clock-maker. Art comes later. A movie must function like clockwork. Not a missing or misshapen piece. Or the clock docsn't work, you see? The alarm doesn't sound.

DUPLAY'S VOICE. You have been criticized for this. It has been –

(She stops the recorder, makes a note.

She rewinds the tape, then hits 'play'.)

LOCKWOOD'S VOICE. – like clockwork. Not a missing or misshapen piece. Or the clock doesn't work, you see?

DUPLAY'S VOICE. You have been criticized for this. It has been said that your movies are nothing but, uh… games, devices to manipulate. That they are not like life. How do you respond to this attitude? An attitude, by the way, I strongly disagree with.

LOCKWOOD'S VOICE. Any artist worth his salt manipulates his audience, Alain. That's a given. To pretend otherwise is disingenuous. The question is how and to what purpose the audience is manipulated. There's got be something going on, you know? Something real.

DUPLAY'S VOICE: Yes, I see.

LOCKWOOD'S VOICE. Real behavior in imaginary circumstances – often rather farfetched circumstances, frankly. That's what I'm after.

(**MIRIAM** *stops the recorder, rewinds.*

She hits 'play'.)

LOCKWOOD'S VOICE. – going on, you know? Something real.

DUPLAY'S VOICE. Yes, I see.

LOCKWOOD'S VOICE. Real behavior in imaginary circumstances – often rather farfetched circumstances, frankly. That's what I'm after.

DUPLAY'S VOICE. This is epitomized for me, I think, in the approach you take with the main character in *Plunder*. A man finds five million pounds on the street, and –

LOCKWOOD'S VOICE. We've spoken of that already, haven't we? Monday or Tuesday?

MIRIAM. Did you?

LOCKWOOD'S VOICE. I thought we had.

DUPLAY'S VOICE. I don't remember that.

MIRIAM. Make up your mind, lads.

LOCKWOOD'S VOICE. I think we did.

DUPLAY'S VOICE. You are sure?

LOCKWOOD'S VOICE. …I'm positive we did. I'll ask Miriam. – Miriam, dear? Are you listening?…

MIRIAM. Yes?

LOCKWOOD'S VOICE. Check the transcripts on that, will you?

MIRIAM. Certainly.

LOCKWOOD'S VOICE. Thank you, dear. Now, Alain, perhaps we should –

(**MIRIAM** *hits 'stop'.*

She flips through one notebook, then another, then another.)

MIRIAM. Oh, damn it all…

(*She rises, exits.*

Silence.

LILIANE BERNARD – *blonde, early 20s, red coat, disheveled, enters. She slowly walks about the room, glancing at this, touching that.*

Sound of door opening and closing.

LILIANE *quickly opens the connecting door to the bedrooms, exits.*

MIRIAM *enters, crosses to the coffee table, flips through the folders resting there.*

She reaches under the coffee table, picks up a worn leather briefcase.)

Alain...

(She takes a quick look inside the briefcase.

She crosses back to the desk, searches among the papers.)

...Where the bloody hell is it?

(She starts briskly for the door.)

I'm losing my mind...

(She exits.

Sound of door opening and closing.

Pause. The connecting door opens, **LILIANE** *enters.*

She moves through the room.

MIRIAM *– notebook in hand – enters, stops.)*

MIRIAM. What are...

(She starts toward **LILIANE***, who sweeps the letter opener off the desk. Pause.)*

I don't know what you think you're doing, but you should put that down. *(Pause.)* Put it down.

(Pause. She steps toward **LILIANE***.*

LILIANE *counters.)*

LILIANE. Where is he?

MIRIAM. Where is – who?

LILIANE. Tell me where he is or I'll kill you!

MIRIAM. I'm sorry, I don't know who you mean. Look, why don't you just –

(She steps toward **LILIANE**.

LILIANE *slices the air with the letter opener.)*

LILIANE. I must talk to him!

(Pause. **MIRIAM** *moves slowly toward* **LILIANE***, who backs away.)*

MIRIAM. Mademoiselle, tell me. Who are you?…Why are you here?…Who is it you want to see?…I can't help you if you won't tell me…So why don't you put that down – and tell me – and we'll try to…We'll try to help you. Yes?…Mademoiselle. If you don't do as I ask I shall contact the hotel manager, who will contact the police, who will have you forcibly removed. They will arrest you and you will go to jail. I shall –

LILIANE. It is not me, Madame, who will go to jail.

MIRIAM. Give me that and then we'll sit down and try to figure out just…just what the problem is…and then we'll –

(She quickly closes the gap between them – **LILIANE'S** *arm flails as she backs away, loses her balance.*

MIRIAM *moves in and grabs* **LILIANE'S** *wrist.*

They fight for the letter opener.

MIRIAM *forces the letter opener out of* **LILIANE'S** *hand.*

LILIANE *pushes* **MIRIAM** *aside, rushes to the balcony as* **MIRIAM** *picks up the letter opener.*

LILIANE *climbs onto the balcony railing. Pause.)*

LILIANE. One more step, Madame, and I jump. *(Pause.)*

MIRIAM. What is you want?

LILIANE. I must see Monsieur Lockwood. *Immediatement.*

MIRIAM. He's…he's not here.

LILIANE. You lie.

MIRIAM. Mademoiselle, believe me: If he were here, you would see him.

LILIANE. I must – I have…It is very important that I –

(She sways.)

MIRIAM. Mademoiselle! Please...please come down...and we'll – we'll wait for him.

LILIANE. No! You will call the police. You will have them take me away! I need to see – I must talk with...

(She sways.)

MIRIAM. I promise you I won't call them. Just please –

LILIANE. – Monsieur Lockwood...The letters...I have the letters...I think I'm going to –

(She sways.

MIRIAM *drops the letter opener, hurries to the balcony.*

She grabs **LILIANE'S** *coat and helps her down.*

She half-carries, half-drags **LILIANE** *toward the couch.)*

...Please...I need to...My head is...spinning... Madame...

(She sinks out of **MIRIAM'S** *grasp to the floor.)*

MIRIAM. Oh, God in Heaven...

(She crosses to **LILIANE.***)*

Mademoiselle, please...Please wake up...Mademoiselle?

(She pats **LILIANE'S** *cheek.)*

Mademoiselle?

(She pats **LILIANE'S** *cheek again.*

LILIANE *groans.*

MIRIAM *drags her to a sitting position.)*

EMMA. *(off)* Miriam?

*(***MIRIAM** *lifts* **LILIANE** *to the couch.)*

EMMA. *(off)* Everything all right?

MIRIAM. Yes, Mrs. Lockwood. Everything's fine.

EMMA. *(off)* I thought I heard something.

MIRIAM. It's nothing, Mrs. Lockwood. Everything's fine.

EMMA. *(off)* That's good. *(Pause.)*

MIRIAM. Wake up, Mademoiselle. Wake up…Oh, why won't you wake up?

(She starts toward the drinks table.

The connecting door opens.)

EMMA *– silk dressing gown over silk pajamas – in connecting doorway.)*

EMMA. I thought I heard something, Miriam. You're sure everything's all right?

MIRIAM. Yes, Mrs. Lockwood.

EMMA. I was sure I'd heard something. *(Pause.)* Mr. Lockwood hasn't called yet?

MIRIAM. Not yet, no.

EMMA. You'll let me know when he does? Even if I've drifted off again?

MIRIAM. Yes, Mrs. Lockwood. *(Pause.)*

EMMA. Very good.

(She exits. Pause.

MIRIAM *starts again for the drinks table.*

EMMA *steps back into the doorway.)*

Even if it's very late you'll call me?

MIRIAM. Yes, Mrs. Lockwood.

EMMA. Very good.

(She exits. Pause.

MIRIAM *crosses to the drinks table.*

She pours a shot of brandy, takes it to **LILIANE**.

She sets the drink aside and rubs **LILIANE'S** *wrists.*

Liliane's eyes flutter.)

LILIANE. What…I…

MIRIAM. Shhh. Drink this.

(She gives **LILIANE** *the shot of brandy.*

LILIANE *drinks.)*

LILIANE. …Where –

MIRIAM. *Shhhh.*

> *(Silence.*
>
> **MIRIAM** *exits through the connecting door...returns.*
>
> *She crosses back toward* **LILIANE.**
>
> *Her path crosses the letter opener.*
>
> *She picks it up, crosses to the desk, sets it down.*
>
> *She crosses to* **LILIANE.***)*

I think she's sleeping again. We must be very quiet. Do you understand?

> *(***LILIANE** *nods.)*

Now. I'm going to ask you to explain your...fantastic behavior. Please keep your voice low. Mrs. Lockwood isn't well and she mustn't be disturbed. Do you understand that?

> *(***LILIANE.** *Nods.)*

MIRIAM. ...Who are you?

LILIANE. My name is Liliane. Liliane Bernard.

MIRIAM. What are you doing here?

LILIANE. I must see Monsieur Lockwood.

MIRIAM. Yes, you've said that. Why must you see Mr. Lockwood?

LILIANE. I will only speak with him.

MIRIAM. I'm Mr. Lockwood's secretary. Anything you'd say to him, you can say to me. *(Pause.)* You'll tell me what you want here, or I shall call the police this instant.

LILIANE. I don't think you want the police to know of this. *(Pause.)*

MIRIAM. We'll see about that.

> *(She crosses to the telephone table.)*

I'm afraid you leave me no other choice.

> *(She picks up the receiver, dials.)*

Bon soir, Antoine. This is Miss Stockton in Room 225. Will you please put me through to the Police?...Yes, the

Police...No, there's nothing for you to worry about...
I'll hold, yes.

LILIANE. Don't talk to the police.

MIRIAM. Will you leave?

LILIANE. No.

MIRIAM. Then I shall tell them to come here and...deal
with you.

LILIANE. And I will tell them how Monsieur Lockwood
attacked me. *(Pause.)*

MIRIAM. ...*Non. C'est rien. Desolé, Monsieur. C'est rien...*

(She replaces the receiver.

Silence.)

LILIANE. Madame...Stockton, it is?...Madame Stockton?
(Pause.) Last year, a friend of mine found a small part
for me in the film of Monsieur Lockwood's. I bring
drinks to the table of the star. A very small scene in the
film, but I am happy, you know, to work with the great
Monsieur Lockwood...One day, when we are done, he
ask me if I have a moment to see him. I say, yes, of
course, you see me now. In private, he says. I want to
discuss something with you. Will you meet me in a little
bit? And in a little bit I go. We meet. And we talk of the
film, and of France, which he says he love very much,
he is always so happy to be here, and how much...how
attractive I am to him. And he kiss me. And I kiss him
back. There is nothing wrong with a few kisses...But
then he says to take off my clothes. He says I will have
more work in the film if I will take off my clothes for
him. He says many girls would like to have the chance
for this, to be in his movie more...I say thank you very
much, but that it not what I want, and that I want to
go. He says it does not matter what you want, and he
starts to be...very rough with me. He makes me to lie
on the bed, he holds me down, he covers my mouth
with his hand, he pulls away my clothes from me, he...

(She begins to cry...

She takes a pack of cigarettes from a coat pocket.

She lights a cigarette, smokes.

Silence.)

MIRIAM. ...When was this?

LILIANE. *Comment?*

MIRIAM. When did this – attack – supposedly happen?

LILIANE. It did happen!

MIRIAM. When?

LILIANE. In October, Madame.

MIRIAM. ...That's almost a year ago. If it happened in October, why are you here *now?*

LILIANE. Circumstances, Madame. The film was done and Monsieur Lockwood returned to the United States shortly after...what happened. He is only back now for the premiere of his film. I couldn't just fly to the United States to see him, could I? *(Pause.)*

MIRIAM. Where did it happen?

LILIANE. Here.

MIRIAM. In this hotel room?

LILIANE. This hotel. He always stays here when he is in Paris.

MIRIAM. ...He does?

LILIANE. You are his secretary, and you don't know that?

MIRIAM. I've...I've only been working for Mr. Lockwood since March.

LILIANE. Ah. I think I know him better than you. *(Pause.)*

MIRIAM. Did anyone see you here?

LILIANE. No, Madame.

MIRIAM. Did you talk to anyone afterwards? Did you go to the police? Did you report this?

LILIANE. I told no one, Madame. I was too ashamed. And I would not have been believed. Monsieur Lockwood is a powerful man. I am...nothing.

MIRIAM. No one else knows?

LILIANE. I swear it, Madame. *(Pause.)*

MIRIAM. You said something about letters.

LILIANE. Yes, Madame. From Monsieur Lockwood.

MIRIAM. Do you have them with you?

LILIANE. One of them, yes.

MIRIAM. May I see it?…Or are you lying about that, too?

LILIANE. I lie about nothing, Madame.

> *(She stubs her cigarette out.*
>
> *She takes an envelope out of a coat pocket.*
>
> **MIRIAM** *crosses to her.*
>
> **LILIANE** *removes a letter from the envelope, holds it out.*
>
> **MIRIAM** *moves closer to read it…too close, evidently:* **LILIANE** *jerks the letter away.)*

MIRIAM. I'm only trying to *read* it, Mademoiselle, not *steal* it.

> *(She crosses to the desk, puts on her glasses, returns to* **LILIANE**.
>
> *She turns on a nearby lamp.*
>
> *She leans forward to read the letter.)*

'My dear Liliane…It must come as a surprise to you to receive this letter after what happened…My fault entirely…You are not to be blamed for what happened…An error, shall we say, in judgment on my part…'

LILIANE. So English, isn't it? 'An error in judgment'.

MIRIAM. …'I feel terrible, and I can only imagine how you must' –

> *(She steps back. Pause.)*

LILIANE. …'Yours – Henry.'

> *(She folds the letter, puts it back in its envelope.)*

MIRIAM. You have others?

LILIANE. Yes, Madame. Two others. *(Pause.)*

MIRIAM. How much do you want for them?

LILIANE. Madame?

MIRIAM. That's why you're here, isn't it? To blackmail Mr. Lockwood? *Pour le chantage*? *(Pause.)*

LILIANE. Madame Stockton, where did you sleep last night?

MIRIAM. I – what has this to do with...

LILIANE. Please. Where did you sleep last night?

MIRIAM. Well, if you must know...I slept here in the hotel. Next door, in fact. My room is right next to the Lockwoods'.

LILIANE. And where did you eat breakfast this morning?

MIRIAM. ...Room service.

LILIANE. Your lunch?

MIRIAM. Mr. Lockwood took a group of us to the Brasserie Lipp.

LILIANE. And dinner?

MIRIAM. Really, Mademoiselle –

LILIANE. Where did you eat your dinner?

MIRIAM. In the hotel.

LILIANE. And where will you sleep tonight? In the hotel? Yes?

MIRIAM. Yes.

LILIANE. You are very lucky, Madame Stockton. A friend of mine in Belleville let me sleep on her floor last night. I have been walking in the streets of Paris all day. I had no breakfast. No lunch. No dinner. I will go to beg this friend to let me sleep on her floor again. She may allow me. She may not. I will not know until I go there and beg. I have not eaten all day and yet I will walk to Belleville tonight...This is what my life is. I see no reason that it will change. I am tired and dirty and hungry, yet no one will help me, no one will do a thing for me but curse me and threaten me with the Police. Always the Police...I have no wish to hurt Monsieur Lockwood. Even with what he has done to me. I would prefer, in fact, never to see him again. But, Madame, I need a place to sleep. I need food to eat. I have no family to help me. I have no one. I have…nothing. Nothing but a few letters…Now tell me, Madame – what would you do if you were in my situation?

(Silence.

MIRIAM *crosses to the desk.)*

MIRIAM. Mr. and Mrs. Lockwood will be out from approximately two o'clock to five o'clock tomorrow afternoon. I suggest you arrive at – let us say…three o'clock. Call from the lobby to make sure that I'm alone. Bring all three letters with you. In exchange for those letters, I will give you five thousand French Francs in cash. Before you receive the money you will sign a document stating that you attempted to blackmail Mr. Lockwood –

LILIANE. But Madame, I did nothing of –

MIRIAM. – that you attempted to blackmail Mr. Lockwood and that the story you told me is completely and utterly false.

LILIANE. It is not!

MIRIAM. You may believe what you like. That is beside the point as far as I am concerned. As long as you make no contact of any kind with Mr. Lockwood in the future, the existence of this document will remain unknown to anyone but me. But if you should in any way – any way at all – attempt to further compromise Mr. Lockwood…Heaven help you. *(Pause.)* Those are the terms. I suggest you accept them. *(Pause.)*

LILIANE. I will be here at three o'clock, Madame.

*(**MIRIAM** opens her purse, removes banknotes.)*

MIRIAM. You'll need some money for a place to sleep tonight and some food. I think twenty Francs will be sufficient.

(She places the money on the desktop.

She crosses to the balcony window.

LILIANE *crosses to the desk, picks up the money.)*

LILIANE. Thank you, Madame.

MIRIAM. Please close the door quietly on your way out.

*(***LILIANE*** starts for the door.*

The telephone rings.

LILIANE *stops.*

MIRIAM *turns.*

The telephone rings.

It rings again.

MIRIAM *crosses to the telephone table.)*

EMMA. *(off)* Miriam?

(The telephone rings again.)

MIRIAM. You've got the money. Now go. Come back tomorrow.

LILIANE. I will, Madame. You may be sure of that.

EMMA. *(off)* Miriam?

(And again.)

MIRIAM. Go!

LILIANE. I want Monsieur Lockwood to see our baby.

EMMA. *(off)* Miriam! Answer the telephone!

*(***LILIANE*** exits.*

The telephone rings again.

And again.

And again.

And again.

And again.

MIRIAM *picks up the receiver.)*

MIRIAM. Hello?…Oh – how…how good of you to check back…No. There's no need to call them, no…I was – upset, and I…Yes…

*(***EMMA*** enters.)*

Of course I understand...I appreciate it. Thank you...
Thank you...Goodnight.

(**MIRIAM** *hangs up.*)

EMMA. Who was that?

MIRIAM. ...Antoine.

EMMA. Why would he be calling us at this hour?

MIRIAM. He...wanted to know if Mr. Lockwood had called.

EMMA. He did? How nice of him.

MIRIAM. Yes.

EMMA. He hasn't called, though, has he?

MIRIAM. Not yet, I'm afraid. No. *(Pause.)*

EMMA. I've been dozing, and I thought he might have
called.

MIRIAM. I'd have let you know, Mrs. Lockwood. *(Pause.)*

EMMA. I hope it went well.

MIRIAM. I'm sure it did. *(Pause.)*

EMMA. Do you think it went well?

MIRIAM. I'm sure it'll be a huge success, Mrs. Lockwood.

EMMA. I'm sure it will be. Our films always are. *(Pause.)*
Miriam, do you think...

MIRIAM. Yes, Mrs. Lockwood?

EMMA. Do you think...on a night like this...a special
night...I might be allowed a glass of wine?

MIRIAM. Mrs. Lockwood, you know what the doctor said
about –

EMMA. Oh, Miriam – don't be so *medical. (Pause.)*

MIRIAM. Well, I suppose on a night like this...

(*She crosses to the drinks table.*

EMMA *crosses to the couch and sits.*)

EMMA. You have a glass, too. You look a little white around
the gills yourself...I'm in such a state, Miriam. Why
doesn't Mr. Lockwood call? He said he'd call the
moment the film was over. I suppose he just hasn't had
time...I do hope it's gone well. He'd be – devastated...

if it didn't. He's so very sensitive, you know, though he doesn't let on that he is. A harsh word destroys him. Mr. Lockwood's on the delicate side. Emotionally. Though looking at him you'd never suspect it. Some people actually think he's a monster. But of course he's not. He just makes movies about monsters, that's all.

(**MIRIAM**, *wineglasses in hand, crosses to* **EMMA.**)

Thank you.

MIRIAM. I think he's one the best, dearest, most wonderful people I've ever met.

EMMA. Miriam, that's lovely. I have to confess that I agree with you, and I applaud your taste and perspicacity... There's a 10-dollar word for you. That's what you get for reading all day.

(*They drink. Pause.*)

MIRIAM. You love him very much, don't you, Mrs. Lockwood?

EMMA. Miriam, I believe if it came right down to it I'd die for him...I so much wanted to be there with him this evening. And I would have been, too, if it weren't for...Well, he knows how I feel. Sometimes, you know, I think I'd kill for that man.

MIRIAM. ...I think I would, too – if necessary. (*Pause.*)

EMMA. You're still working?

MIRIAM. Oh, yes. Yes. But I've been taking a little break.

EMMA. Don't let me stop you. I know Alain wants that tape done by tomorrow. Will you have it finished by then?

MIRIAM. I'm almost done.

EMMA. You could finish it while we're waiting. (*Pause.*) Don't mind me. I'll be quiet as a bug.

MIRIAM. Well...All right...Yes, I'll...

(*She crosses to the desk, sits.*

She opens her notebook.)

EMMA. What do you think of Monsieur Duplay?

MIRIAM. Alain? He's awfully nice, isn't he?

EMMA. He is. But you should read his articles. Monsieur Duplay can be an exceptionally vicious critic. He throws roses at one's feet – or vitriol in one's face...He wants to direct movies, you know.

MIRIAM. Don't they all?

EMMA. But no one will give him the money. He has *enemies*... It's very sad. He's quite passionate on the subject.

MIRIAM. He would be, wouldn't he?

EMMA. Yes, he's quite passionate – and quite handsome.

MIRIAM. Handsome?...I suppose so.

EMMA. Don't you think he is?

MIRIAM. Oh, I'm not much of a judge, I'm afraid. Of male beauty.

EMMA. I think he's perfectly ravishing. I'm smitten, Miriam – no two ways about it, and I don't give a tinker's dam who knows it. *(Pause.)* He's interested, Miriam. I think you should do something about it.

MIRIAM. Well...He has asked me out.

EMMA. I didn't know that! When was this?

MIRIAM. The other day.

EMMA. What did you tell him?

MIRIAM. I said maybe.

EMMA. Good. That way he won't think you're too eager. *(Pause.)* Where does he want to take you?

MIRIAM. To the movies. *(Pause.)* And do you know something, Mrs. Lockwood?...I think I'll go.

EMMA. I knew you were a smart girl. You don't run into something like that every day, and more's the pity. *(Pause.)* He's got one flaw, though, Alain.

MIRIAM. What's that?

EMMA. He'd forget his head if it weren't sewn on. But other than that...

*(**MIRIAM** picks up a pen, turns on the reel-to-reel recorder.)*

LOCKWOOD'S VOICE. – move onto another question... What's that you've got written there?

DUPLAY'S VOICE. 'Fear'. The word 'fear.'

(**LOCKWOOD** *laughs.*)

DUPLAY'S VOICE. Why do you laugh?

LOCKWOOD'S VOICE. Because it's like talking about an old friend.

DUPLAY'S VOICE. You know each other well?

LOCKWOOD'S VOICE. Intimately, Alain...Intimately. I've spent a great deal of time in his company and have come to the conclusion that fear is a noble emotion – but only in the movie-house. In film fear is my bread-and-butter.

DUPLAY'S VOICE. And in life?

LOCKWOOD'S VOICE. Life is –

(**MIRIAM** *shuts the recorder off. Pause.*

She rewinds the tape.)

DUPLAY'S VOICE. – each other well?

LOCKWOOD'S VOICE. Intimately, Alain...Intimately. I've spent a great deal of time in his company and have come to the conclusion that fear is a noble emotion – but only in the movie-house. In film fear is my bread-and-butter.

DUPLAY'S VOICE. And in life?

LOCKWOOD'S VOICE. Life is another thing altogether. Much more frightening than one of my films...

(**LOCKWOOD** *bursts into laughter.*)

EMMA. Miriam?

LOCKWOOD'S VOICE. – Much more frightening.

(**MIRIAM** *turns the recorder off.*)

EMMA. I didn't know you smoked.

MIRIAM. I don't.

EMMA. Well, that's curious. There's a cigarette in the ash-tray here. (*Pause.*)

MIRIAM. I smoke every once in a while. When I'm – when I'm worried.

EMMA. What are you worried about?

MIRIAM. Mr. Lockwood's movie.

EMMA. Oh, there's nothing to worry about there. I'm sure they'll love it…Though I wish he'd call.

(*Pause.* MIRIAM *switches on the recorder.*

Sound of LOCKWOOD *laughing.*

She stops the tape.

She rewinds.

She hits 'play'.)

LOCKWOOD'S VOICE. – a noble emotion – but only in the movie-house. In film fear is my bread-and-butter.

DUPLAY'S VOICE. And in life?

LOCKWOOD'S VOICE. Life is another thing altogether. Much more frightening than one of my films…

(LOCKWOOD *laughs.*)

Much more frightening…

(MIRIAM *turns the recorder off.*

She puts her head in her hands.

Silence.)

EMMA. Miriam, are you –

(*The telephone rings.*

MIRIAM *jolts upright.*)

EMMA. I'll bet that's him. Answer it, Miriam. Answer it!

(MIRIAM *rises.*

The telephone rings again.

She crosses to the telephone table, picks up the receiver.)

MIRIAM. Hello?…Yes, Mr. Lockwood. She's right here. Just a moment.

(*She lifts up the telephone, carries it to* EMMA, *hands her the receiver.*)

EMMA. Henry? How was it?…Oh. Oh, I'm so glad…They did?

(She turns to **MIRIAM***.)*

They cheered at the end. – What?…No! They didn't!

(She turns to **MIRIAM***.)*

Standing ovation…Oh, I'm so happy…I'll try, but I don't see how I can. I'm just too excited!…I'm not a bit tired. I feel like I could dance all night!…Who was there?…Audrey and Mel?…

(She turns to **MIRIAM***.)*

Audrey and Mel were there…How was she dressed?… No kidding? I didn't know Marcello was in town… Really? What did he think? Did you talk with him?… Well, Orson would say that, wouldn't he?…Who else?…Simone? With or without Yves?…Did she like the film?…Tell me all about it later. I know you have to make the rounds…All right…Yes…Yes, I will…I love you, too. Come home soon. I miss you…Always…

(She holds out the telephone to **MIRIAM***.)*

Miriam, I think another glass of wine is in order.

MIRIAM. Yes, Mrs. Lockwood.

(She takes the telephone from **EMMA***.)*

EMMA. I'm so relieved, I can't tell you. Not so much for me as for him. *I* know a good movie when I see one. But Mr. Lockwood gets *so* wrought-up.

*(***MIRIAM** *crosses to the telephone table, replaces the telephone.)*

You know what it's like, Miriam? A night like tonight?

MIRIAM. What, Mrs. Lockwood?

(She crosses to the drinks table.)

EMMA. I'll tell you exactly what it's like. It's exactly like the very first time a mother and father show their baby to the world.

(**MIRIAM'S** *hand jerks and the wine bottle crashes into the other bottles on the drinks table.*)

EMMA. *(Continued)* Miriam! You're nervous as a cat!

MIRIAM. I'm sorry, Mrs. Lockwood.

EMMA. Smash them all, I don't care. Tonight I don't give a damn. We're a roaring success and I want the world to know!

(**MIRIAM** *starts wiping up spilled wine.*)

Leave that for later, Miriam. Don't be so – *quotidian.* We've had our trial by fire and the worst is over.

(**MIRIAM**, *wine bottle in hand, crosses to* **EMMA** *and fills her glass, then her own.*)

Isn't that so?

MIRIAM. Yes, Mrs. Lockwood. I hope so.

EMMA. …Goodness, how could I have forgotten? A toast, Miriam – we need a toast.

(**MIRIAM** *lifts her glass.*)

MIRIAM. To "Panic."

(**EMMA** *lifts her glass.*)

EMMA. To Henry Lockwood's "Panic."

(*Lights fade.*)

3.

(Darkness.

Lights up.

Curtains drawn.

A cigarette burns in an ashtray.

A clock chimes the hour: four o'clock.

Sound of door opening.

Sound of door closing.

MIRIAM *enters from the foyer.*

She sits, picks up the cigarette, smokes.

She rises, crosses to balcony, opens drapes, looks down at street.

She sits, smokes.

She grinds out the cigarette.

She rises, crosses to the desk, picks up the telephone...puts it down.

She sits.

Sound of door opening.

MIRIAM *turns.*

She starts for the door.)

MIRIAM. Where have you been? I've been waiting –

(Duplay – in white trench coat – enters.

MIRIAM *stops. Pause.)*

DUPLAY. *Salut.*

MIRIAM. Alain...Hello. *(Pause.)* I'm afraid Mr. Lockwood's out. He and Mrs. Lockwood –

DUPLAY. – are at the American Hospital. I know. *(Pause.)*

MIRIAM. I'll tell him you stopped by.

DUPLAY. It isn't Monsieur Lockwood I have come to see. *(Pause.)* I want to talk to you, Miriam.

MIRIAM. I don't really have the time right now to talk, I'm afraid. I was – I was –

DUPLAY. Sit down, please.

MIRIAM. I've got to go to the post office to mail a few things, so perhaps if you'd care to –

DUPLAY. Has she been here yet? Or are you still waiting for her? *(Pause.)*

MIRIAM. I'm not waiting for anyone.

DUPLAY. *Ma chere* Miriam, you are a terrible liar. I know Liliane Bernard was here last night. Perhaps together we can figure out what to do about this...situation. *(Pause.)*

(**MIRIAM** *sits. Pause.)*

MIRIAM. How much do you know?

DUPLAY. Enough to know that Monsieur Lockwood is in serious trouble. And that we must help him – if we can. I want to help him, Miriam. I think we both do. *(Pause.)*

MIRIAM. How did you find out?

DUPLAY. She told me.

MIRIAM. You *know* her?

DUPLAY. Not well, no. Liliane once worked for a few months in the office of the *Carnet Du Cinema*. I helped her out a little bit every now and then. Lunch, a coffee, you know...I was nice to her, simple as that, and I don't think many people had been...She was fired for stealing. I hadn't seen her, hadn't thought about her in years – till around two o'clock this morning...She was waiting at my building when I came back from the premiere. I didn't recognize her at first, she was so changed, so...troubled. I tried to find out what was wrong, but she was not too clear in her mind. She kept saying that Monsieur Lockwood had done something to her. Something awful...I didn't know what to make of it. I mean, there have been rumors in the past about Monsieur Lockwood...But only rumors. I don't believe them.

MIRIAM. *I* don't. *(Pause.)* What else did she tell you?

DUPLAY. She said she'd been to see you and that you were going to help her in some way, or you had helped her, or something…She talked about a letter. Or letters. I'm not sure which. It was not easy to understand her. Do you know what she meant?

MIRIAM. Mr. Lockwood wrote her a number of letters concerning the…incident.

DUPLAY. Did she show them to you?

MIRIAM. One of them, yes.

DUPLAY. And?

MIRIAM. It corroborates what she told me.

DUPLAY. May I see this letter?

MIRIAM. I don't have it. I don't have any of them.

DUPLAY. She says you bought them from her.

MIRIAM. No!…That's why she was coming here today. I was going to buy them and destroy them – put an end to the whole business. But she didn't show up…Or hasn't yet. I've been waiting here all afternoon. Waiting and going out of my mind.

DUPLAY. …You don't have the letters?

MIRIAM. No. I wish I did. *(Pause.)* Didn't she show them to you?

DUPLAY. I left the room for a minute and when I came back, she was gone.

MIRIAM. – What?

DUPLAY. Like smoke.

MIRIAM. Well, where did she *go?*

DUPLAY. Miriam, if I knew that, we'd have the letters now.

(**MIRIAM** *rises, crosses to balcony window, peers through curtains.*)

MIRIAM. We've got to find her, Alain. We've got to get those letters. Without them, her story isn't worth a damn. With them…

DUPLAY. She could destroy Monsieur Lockwood.

MIRIAM. And Mrs. Lockwood. This would kill her. Without

a doubt. This would kill her.

DUPLAY. It might kill Liliane, too. *(Pause.)* Desperate. Unhappy. No money. No family, no one to help...

(He picks up the letter opener on the desk.)

Many girls kill themselves with less reason than that.

(Pause. He sets the letter opener down.)

MIRIAM. Will you help me?

DUPLAY. But of course, Miriam.

(He crosses to her.)

I'll do whatever I can. Which is probably not much, but...Of course I'll help you.

(He places his hand on her arm.)

I think there is nothing I wouldn't do for you...And the Lockwoods.

MIRIAM. Alain, this has got me so...I'm so worried about...

(He puts his arms around her.)

DUPLAY. Everything will be all right, Miriam. I swear to that.

MIRIAM. We've got to find her!

DUPLAY. We will.

MIRIAM. But how?

DUPLAY. Perhaps she'll come back.

MIRIAM. You expect her to just walk in through the door?

DUPLAY. I don't know, Miriam. But we will find her...Just as I have found you.

MIRIAM. Alain, you –

DUPLAY. Shhhhh.

(He kisses her.

Sound of door opening.

They separate.

Sound of door closing.

LOCKWOOD *and* **EMMA** *– in a red coat – enter.)*

EMMA. Miriam! Alain! Hello. Hello.

MIRIAM. Mrs. Lockwood.

DUPLAY. Madame. Monsieur Lockwood.

EMMA. Look what Henry bought me, Miriam!

LOCKWOOD. Hello, Alain. Miriam.

EMMA. Isn't it lovely?

DUPLAY. Beautiful, Madame.

MIRIAM. Mr. Lockwood.

EMMA. It's a tradition, you know. The morning after a film opens, I get a new coat.

LOCKWOOD. For services rendered.

EMMA. He always says that.

MIRIAM. It's gorgeous, Mrs. Lockwood.

EMMA. Feel the fabric, Miriam

(MIRIAM crosses to EMMA.

DUPLAY crosses to LOCKWOOD.)

DUPLAY. How was the visit with the doctor?

(LOCKWOOD shakes his head.)

MIRIAM. It's so soft, Mrs. Lockwood.

EMMA. I know. I'm wearing it out to dinner this evening. Where are we going, Henry?

LOCKWOOD. Fouquet's.

EMMA. Wonderful. Look at the pockets, Miriam. – The trip to the doctor was fine, Alain. No change. I'm not much better –

LOCKWOOD. Emma, that's not what –

EMMA. I hear everything, Henry. Don't fool yourself. – Would you open the curtains, Miriam? It's so gloomy in here.

MIRIAM. Yes, Mrs. Lockwood.

(She crosses to the curtains.)

EMMA. Not much better, the doctor said, but at least no worse.

DUPLAY. But lovely as ever.

EMMA. *Monsieur, vous-etes trop gentil – mais merci, quand-meme.*

*(**MIRIAM** opens the curtains and sun floods in.)*

EMMA. That's more like it. Thank you, Miriam.

(She walks into a pool of sunlight.)

…Oh, that feels so wonderful…Henry?…Come here a moment, would you?

*(**LOCKWOOD** crosses to **EMMA**. Pause.)*

What does this remind you of? *(Pause.)*

LOCKWOOD. Amalfi…1928.

(Silence.

Lights fade.)

4.

(Darkness.

Dim streelight through windows.)

LOCKWOOD'S VOICE. This will show you what I mean.

(A square of white and the clatter of a 16-mm projector.

Numbers: 10...9...8...7...6...5...4...3...2...1...0

*Film: a sequence from one of **LOCKWOOD'S** movies: a man is pursued through a theatre during a performance.*

The film ends.

EMMA, **MIRIAM** *and* **DUPLAY** *applaud.)*

LOCKWOOD'S VOICE. ...Bob was quite good in that, wasn't he?

EMMA'S VOICE. Where did you shoot that, Henry? Was it the Longacre?

LOCKWOOD'S VOICE. I think it was. Wasn't it?

EMMA'S VOICE. No, it wasn't. I remember now...It was a theatre somewhere in the West 30s. They tore it down recently.

MIRIAM'S VOICE. The Glenhurst?

LOCKWOOD'S VOICE. It could have been. I really don't remember. All I recall, really, is the fact that we had to buy out the theatre for three days. David was not a bit happy about spending the money for that...It might have been the Glenhurst. I don't know.

DUPLAY'S VOICE. The studio records say it was the Harlequin Theatre on West 38th.

LOCKWOOD'S VOICE. Well, there you have it. I could have shot it on a soundstage for all it matters. The point, you see, was to create something that can't be done in a book or on a stage. Something uniquely cinematic. A sequence like that speaks for itself. No explanation needed. You'll have noticed that –

JULIET'S VOICE. Some things must be explained, Monsieur.

(JULIET COLLARD – brunette, chic gray suit, hat and gloves, spectacles – steps into the projector light.)

LOCKWOOD. Who are you?

JULIET. My name is Juliet Cottard. No, you don't know me. But I know who you are, Monsieur Henry Allen Lockwood – and I know what you have done.

LOCKWOOD. What are you doing here? What do you want?

JULIET. Liliane Bernard was my sister. I want to know why you murdered her.

(She raises a hand into the projector light.

The hand holds a gun.)

And then – perhaps – I will murder you.

*(Pause. **DUPLAY** springs at **JULIET**.*

Gunshot and blackout.)

ACT II

1.

(Darkness.

Telephone rings.

Rings again.

Rings again.

Lights up.

DUPLAY *– at desk – unloads the gun.*

MIRIAM *and* **JULIET**, *standing near couch.*

EMMA, *seated.*

LOCKWOOD *on telephone.)*

LOCKWOOD. …I understand…Yes…Naturally you would, yes…Your guess is as good as mine, Antoine…A truck, perhaps – *un camion*…No, there's no need for that… No…I think we understand each other…I value your discretion…Mrs. Lockwood's condition, you know… Yes…Thank you…You as well…

(He replaces the receiver.)

DUPLAY. Monsieur Lockwood?

LOCKWOOD. Yes, Alain?

DUPLAY. …What I should I do with this?

LOCKWOOD. Put it in the drawer, please, for the moment. Top right.

*(**DUPLAY** places the gun and bullets in the drawer.)*

Lock it if you would, and *donnez-moi le clé.*

*(**DUPLAY** locks the drawer, crosses to **LOCKWOOD** with the key.*

LOCKWOOD *approaches* **JULIET**.*)*

Look closely, Mademoiselle. Do you see this? Do you know what it is? *(Pause.)* This, Mademoiselle, is the key to your future. I don't know who you are, why you're here or what you're after. But I'll tell you this: Should you ever impose yourself upon me again, I shall unlock that drawer, give that gun to the Police and tell them how you tried to kill me. *Comprenez-vous*, Mademoiselle? *(Pause.)*

JULIET. Then we may both go to jail, Monsieur Lockwood. You have the gun…I have the letters.

(She starts for the door.)

DUPLAY. Miriam, she has the –

(Juliet stops. Pause.)

EMMA. What do you mean, Alain?

DUPLAY. …Nothing, Madame Lockwood. Nothing at all.

EMMA. Miriam? What are these letters the young lady's talking about?

MIRIAM. I – I don't know, Mrs. Lockwood. *(Pause.)*

EMMA. Henry – do you?

LOCKWOOD. I haven't the faintest idea.

EMMA. Then I'll have to find out for myself, won't I?

(She rises.)

Mademoiselle, will you please be seated?

DUPLAY. Madame Lockwood, this young woman is not to be believed!

EMMA. Then it won't matter what she tells me, will it?

LOCKWOOD. Emma, I forbid you to speak to her!

EMMA. And why is that, Henry?

LOCKWOOD. She tried to kill me!

EMMA. Then we should call the Police, don't you think?

LOCKWOOD. It's not necessary.

EMMA. What's this all about, Henry? Why don't you want me to talk to her?

MIRIAM. Mrs. Lockwood, please don't excite yourself.

LOCKWOOD. Get her out of here, Alain.

DUPLAY. Of course.

*(He starts toward **JULIET**.)*

EMMA. You'll do no such thing. You're all trying to pull the wool over my eyes, and I won't have it! I want to know what's going on here!

DUPLAY. Monsieur Lockwood...

LOCKWOOD. Go on, Alain.

EMMA. You may be able to tell everyone else what to do, but I won't stand for it, Henry.

LOCKWOOD. You'll do what I say.

EMMA. I will not!

LOCKWOOD. Emma...

(Silence.)

EMMA. I'm – I'm sorry...Miriam, please don't think that I...I'm...

(Pause. She sits.)

MIRIAM. Mrs. Lockwood, are you all right?

LOCKWOOD. What is it, Emma?

EMMA. It's nothing.

LOCKWOOD. Is it your heart?

MIRIAM. Shall I call the doctor?

EMMA. I'll be fine. I'll be fine. Really. Just...

LOCKWOOD. Miriam, get Mrs. Lockwood's medicine.

MIRIAM. Right away.

(She exits.)

LOCKWOOD. Are you sure you're all right? Should I call the doctor?

EMMA. You're making far too much of this, Henry.

LOCKWOOD. He could be here in a moment.

EMMA. I don't need a doctor.

LOCKWOOD. Let me be the judge of that.

DUPLAY. It might be the wise thing to do, Madame Lock-wood.

LOCKWOOD. Miriam? Where are you?

(**MIRIAM** – *medicine bottle in hand* – *enters.*)

MIRIAM. I'm right here, Mr. Lockwood.

(**LOCKWOOD** *crosses to her, takes the medicine bottle.*)

LOCKWOOD. Thank you, Miriam.

(*He crosses to the drinks table, prepares* **EMMA'S** *medicine.*)

EMMA. I'm sorry, Henry. I didn't mean to…to get so…

LOCKWOOD. It's all my fault, mother. I shouldn't have spoken to you like that.

EMMA. I shouldn't have, either.

LOCKWOOD. You see, that's what I've been trying to tell you. You've got to be careful. You mustn't get excited. You mustn't over-exert yourself. You've got to take it easy.

EMMA. But I don't want to.

LOCKWOOD. We all have to do things we don't like sometimes.

EMMA. I should listen to you, shouldn't I?

LOCKWOOD. You should, but you don't.

(*Glass of medicine in hand, he crosses to Emma.*)

EMMA. And do you know why that is?

LOCKWOOD. Why is that?

EMMA. Because it's not you I want to listen to – it's that young woman.

LOCKWOOD. Oh for God's *sake*, Emma.

MIRIAM. Mrs. Lockwood? Please take your medicine.

EMMA. I don't want it.

MIRIAM. Mrs. Lockwood, please.

LOCKWOOD. Alain, will you…

EMMA. I tell you I don't *want* it.

(**DUPLAY** *starts toward* **JULIET**.)

LOCKWOOD. Take your medicine, Emma – now.

EMMA. But I don't –

LOCKWOOD. *Now.*

(**EMMA** *takes the glass.*)

DUPLAY. *On y va. Vite.*

MIRIAM. Should I call the hotel doctor?

EMMA. I don't *need* him, Miriam. I'm fine.

JULIET. *Mais les lettres – J'ai les lettres –*

(**DUPLAY** *takes* **JULIET'S** *arm and steers her toward the door*)

DUPLAY. *Depechez-vous. Maintenant.*

MIRIAM. Mrs. Lockwood, you've got to drink your –

EMMA. Alain, what are you doing?

(**DUPLAY** *stops*)

DUPLAY. …What Monsieur Lockwood has asked, Madame.

EMMA. Bring the young lady over here.

LOCKWOOD. Emma, you're in no condition for any –

EMMA. Let me be the judge of that.

MIRIAM. Please take your medicine, Mrs. Lockwood.

EMMA. I won't drink a drop of it until Alain does what I ask.

LOCKWOOD. Are you trying to kill yourself? Because that's what –

EMMA. Henry – if you want me to drop dead with *frustration*, this is a Goddamned good way to go about it. Something's going on here and I'm not going to take it *easy*, I'm not going to be *careful*, and I'm fully capable of *over-exerting* myself until I find out exactly what it is. And I'm not taking my medicine until Mademoiselle –

JULIET. Cottard, Madame, Juliet Cottard.

EMMA. Until Mademoiselle Cottard has had a chance to explain herself. *(Pause.)*

LOCKWOOD. You'll take your medicine?

EMMA. Yes. *(Pause.)*

LOCKWOOD. All right. All right...Alain.

> (**DUPLAY** *and* **JULIET** *move to the couch.*
>
> **JULIET** *sits.*)

EMMA. Young woman, you've made a very serious accusation against my husband.

JULIET. I know that, Madame.

EMMA. You claim he murdered your sister?

JULIET. Yes.

MIRIAM. Your medicine, Mrs. Lockwood.

EMMA. Do you have any kind of proof to substantiate this claim?

LOCKWOOD. No!

JULIET. I...It is a...

EMMA. It's a simple question, is what is. Do you – or do you not – have any kind of proof?

LOCKWOOD. How could she?

DUPLAY. It is utterly absurd!

EMMA. Do you?

JULIET. ...No.

LOCKWOOD. Alain – get this girl out of here.

> (**DUPLAY** *crosses toward Juliet.*)

MIRIAM. Mrs. Lockwood, please drink your –

JULIET. All I have are the letters Monsieur Lockwood wrote to my sister after he raped her.

> (**DUPLAY** *stops.*
>
> *Everything stops.*
>
> *Silence.*
>
> **EMMA** *slowly raises the glass of medicine to her lips, drinks...*
>
> *Holds out the glass to* **MIRIAM**. *Pause.*
>
> **MIRIAM** *takes it, walks slowly to the drinks table.*

EMMA. ...Raped her?

JULIET. Yes, Madame. Rape. *(Pause.)* The letters arrived in this afternoon's post. With a note from Liliane that told me what they were and why I was to have them. She must have known...Must have had some idea of what was going to happen. She always had strong – feelings...*premonitions*...Why else would she have sent them to me? And something did happen. The most awful thing. The Police called me a little after six o'clock. They told me my sister was dead. But how could that be? I'd just received a note from her. You must be mistaken, I said. The man I spoke to said – 'I hope we are'...They asked me to come and look at the body. All the way there I told myself, 'They are wrong, they must be. They have to be. Liliane isn't dead. She can't be. It won't be her. It won't be her.' But when I saw the body – the red coat – I knew it *was* her. She loved that coat...You gave it to her.

EMMA. Henry...

LOCKWOOD. I never *met* the girl!

JULIET. You know what you did, Monsieur. You know. Her face...Her beautiful face...Oh God, what you've done!

(She begins to cry.)

She was so pretty...So pretty...What they showed me, the Police – was not. Oh, God...God...

(She cries.

DUPLAY *crosses to the telephone table, picks up the receiver.)*

LOCKWOOD. What are you doing, Alain?

ALAIN. Getting to the bottom of these lies – if I can... Antoine? Ah, *pardon* – *Henri. Je voudrais parler avec la Police...Non, non, tout va bien...Bon soir. Inspecteur Passavant, s'il vous plaît...Oui. J'attends...*

(MIRIAM *crosses to the desk, picks up desk telephone.)*

MIRIAM. I want to hear this.

DUPLAY. A good idea, Miriam...I met Passavant through Jean-Pierre Melville. I have no doubt that he – *'Allo, Marcel? C'est Alain Duplay. Sais-tu si le corps d'une femme – une jeune femme avec un manteau rouge – a ete enregistre dernierment?*

(He turns to **LOCKWOOD***.)*

He's checking now...*Oui, Marcel?*...A body was taken from the Seine early this morning.

EMMA. Oh Lord.

MIRIAM. The coat. Ask about the coat.

DUPLAY. *Le manteau rouge, Marcel? Elle etait – ...Je vois...T'es sure?...*

JULIET. I told you!

MIRIAM. Ask if they know anything else.

DUPLAY. *Qu'est-ce que t'as comme informations sur elle?...Oui? Ah bon.*

MIRIAM. Hold on a moment, Alain.

(She uncaps a foutain pen, finds a notepad to write on.)

Go ahead.

DUPLAY. *Marcel? Je suis pret...Nom: Bernard. Prenom: Liliane. Age: vingt-deux ans. Cause du deces: Fracture cranienne... Est-ce que son corps a ete identifie?...Par qui?...Sa soeur. Comment s'apelle t-elle?...Juliet Cottard...Je vois, Je vois...Je peux pas...Mille Merci. A charge de revanche, Marcel.*

(He turns to **LOCKWOOD***.)*

Would you like to speak with the Inspector?

*(***LOCKWOOD*** *shakes his head.)*

Marcel? Merci encore...C'est vrai, oui...Salut.

(He hangs up. Pause.)

LOCKWOOD. What did he tell you?...Alain? *(Pause.)*

MIRIAM. Name: Liliane Bernard. Age: 22. Cause Of Death: Skull fracture. Her body was identified by her sister, Juliet Cottard. *(Pause.)* It doesn't *prove* anything. Only that her body has been...found. *(Pause.)* You have my condolences, Mademoiselle.

JULIET. I had not seen her or talked with her in almost a year. To be...brought together...in this way is...beyond belief.

(*MIRIAM* turns to **DUPLAY**.)

MIRIAM. I should have made sure she found a room last night, somewhere she'd be safe.

DUPLAY. Please, this is not the –

EMMA. I don't understand, Miriam. Are you saying you *saw* this young woman's sister last night?

MIRIAM. ...Yes, Mrs. Lockwood.

EMMA. Here? In this hotel room? – And you didn't *tell* me?

LOCKWOOD. Miriam, is this true?

MIRIAM. Yes. Yes it is. She came here while I was working last night. On the transcripts. She showed me one of the letters. It was...I didn't know what to make of it, so I...I told her I'd buy them from her. I was going to buy them – secretly – and...burn them. So you and Mr. Lockwood would never have to know.

EMMA. I wish you'd come to me. We might have been able to avoid all of this. How, I don't know, but...You should have told me.

MIRIAM. I'm sorry, Mrs. Lockwood.

EMMA. If I'd just had a chance to talk with that young woman...

DUPLAY. Miriam was only trying to protect you, Madame Lockwood.

EMMA. I understand that, Alain. I'm not blaming her. – I'm not blaming you, Miriam. Please don't think that. I'm not blaming you.

MIRIAM. Mrs. Lockwood, all I wanted was...I was trying... I couldn't bear it if anything were to happen to Mr. Lockwood. Or to you. I think so much of both of you that...perhaps I...

LOCKWOOD. You did what you thought best, Miriam. I appreciate it greatly.

MIRIAM. That's all I…all I tried to do…If that was wrong…

(*She rises.*)

Excuse me.

(*She exits. Pause.*

DUPLAY *rises.*)

DUPLAY. I will make sure she is all right.

(*He starts for the door.*)

EMMA. First I think you should tell us what's going on here between you and Miriam.

(DUPLAY *stops.*

He crosses back into the room.)

DUPLAY. Madame Lockwood, you have caught me out. I too saw Liliane Bernard last night.

LOCKWOOD. What?

EMMA. Why would she come to you?

LOCKWOOD. When was this?

DUPLAY. After the premiere. As for why she should come to me, I am not really sure. I think, Madame, she came because – I think this is true – because I was kind to her once.

EMMA. What did you do?

DUPLAY. It was when she worked for a while at the magazine.

LOCKWOOD. The *Carnet Du Cinema*?

DUPLAY. The *Carnet*, yes. She was very poor and I would buy her a coffee or a sandwich every now and then… Say 'hello' to her in the hall…She did not work there long. She left the magazine under a cloud, as they say.

EMMA. Can you tell us why?

DUPLAY. It is a matter of some delicacy, Madame. The official story was that she stole money from the office. But that is not it – or all of it…

LOCKWOOD. Go on.

DUPLAY. She…Well, yes, she did take money. But the reason she took it is the real scandal. Evidently, there was – there is a child…It was an unpleasant situation.

EMMA. And you say times have changed, Henry?

LOCKWOOD. Did she tell you anything about all this? When you saw her last night?

DUPLAY. No. Not a thing. I could see she was…distraught. Is that the word?…But before I could find out why, she had disappeared. I had gone into the other room, and when I came back – she was gone.

EMMA. She said nothing about the letters or…

DUPLAY. No, Madame. I assure you of that.

(He starts for the door, stops.)

DUPLAY. I am sorry that I said nothing sooner. Miriam and I – we are only trying to help you. To help you both. We feel that…well…I think it is clear how we feel. *(Pause.)* I will see about Miriam now.

(He crosses to the door, stops.)

I would give my life to make this situation different.

LOCKWOOD. Thank you, Alain.

EMMA. And thank you for telling us.

(He exits.

Silence.)

EMMA. …What *are* we going to do about this, Henry?

LOCKWOOD. Nothing. It's a pack of lies.

JULIET. My sister is dead, Monsieur. That is not a lie. That is a fact. And I think you are the reason she is dead.

LOCKWOOD. Mademoiselle Cottard, I'm terribly sorry about your sister. You have my deepest sympathies. But you must understand this: I didn't kill her. I am not a murderer.

JULIET. You are a fine actor, Monsieur. You should be in the movies.

LOCKWOOD. Emma, please – make this young woman listen to reason.

JULIET. You forced yourself on her.

LOCKWOOD. I did not.

JULIET. You wrote her letters.

LOCKWOOD. I did not!

JULIET. And then to shut her mouth, you wrapped your hands around her throat –

LOCKWOOD. I deny that!

JULIET. You felt her warm flesh beneath your fingers –

LOCKWOOD. You lying bitch!

JULIET. Did you call her names, too? Is that what you like? To call them names? Make them crawl on the ground? Make them licks your boots before you fuck them? Before you kill them? Before you –

(**LOCKWOOD** *slaps her.*

Silence.

LOCKWOOD *crosses to the drinks table, pours himself a brandy, drinks.*)

EMMA. ...I think you owe Mademoiselle Cottard an apology, Henry. *(Pause.)* Henry? *(Pause.)*

LOCKWOOD. I apologize.

(*Silence.*

MIRIAM, *followed by* **DUPLAY**, *enters.*)

EMMA. How are you feeling, my dear? Better?

MIRIAM. Much better, thank you. I don't know what came over me.

EMMA. Please be seated. Both of you.

(**MIRIAM** *and* **DUPLAY** *sit.*)

Mademoiselle, do you have the letters with you?

JULIET. ...Yes. One of them. And the note from Liliane.

EMMA. May I see them?

(*Pause.* **JULIET** *takes an envelope out of her purse.*

She removes the note from the envelope.)

JULIET. Don't try to take it. It wouldn't do any good.

EMMA. If you'll simply place it on the table, I don't even have to touch it.

JULIET. Yes, all right...

(She places the note on the coffee table.

EMMA *leans forward, peers at it.*

MIRIAM *and Duplay cross to the coffee table, look at the note.)*

EMMA. And the letter?

(JULIET takes the note, puts it in the envelope.

She takes a letter from the envelope, unfolds it, places it on the coffee table.

EMMA *and* **MIRIAM** *and* **DUPLAY** *study the letter.)*

...Henry, would you look at this, please?

(LOCKWOOD crosses to the coffee table, reads...walks away.)

...Thank you, Mademoiselle.

(JULIET puts the letter back into its envelope.)

Whatever else you may or may not be – a murderer or only a man unjustly accused of murder – one thing is undeniable...Your handwriting.

LOCKWOOD. What do you mean?

EMMA. After all these years, I know your handwriting as well as I know my own, Henry. You wrote those letters.

LOCKWOOD. Someone must have forged them.

EMMA. Miriam, perhaps? That's our stationery. Are you accusing Miriam? Or Alain?

LOCKWOOD. Don't be ridiculous.

EMMA. Miriam, you know Mr. Lockwood's handwriting, don't you?

MIRIAM. I...I see it practically every day. I should think I do.

EMMA. Would you say this letter was composed in Mr. Lockwood's hand?

DUPLAY. Madame Lockwood, it has to be a forgery. That is the only explanation.

EMMA. Answer the question, Miriam. *(Pause.)*

MIRIAM. Yes. It's Mr. Lockwood's handwriting.

JULIET. You see? Even your friends must say the truth when it appears!

DUPLAY. Shut your mouth!

EMMA. Henry, you wrote this, didn't you?

(Silence.)

LOCKWOOD. ...If you say I did, I must have. *(Pause.)* The handwriting and all. *(Pause.)* But here's the thing, you see...I don't remember writing that letter.

JULIET. Please, Monsieur!

LOCKWOOD. That's the absolute truth, Emma. I honestly have no memory of writing that letter – or any other letters, for that matter.

EMMA. That's awfully convenient, Henry.

LOCKWOOD. Emma, I don't even remember *meeting* this Liliane Bernard in the first place.

MIRIAM. But you must have. She's in your...

EMMA. Yes, Miriam? *(Pause.)*

MIRIAM. She's in your film. She told me that. She – she brings drinks to the table at the casino.

JULIET. First you forget the letters, now you forget your film! *(Pause.)*

LOCKWOOD. That's not Liliane Bernard. The actress who plays that is...What is her name?...Alain – a stage actress. Tall, thin, red hair. Works at the Francaise. She was in the Clement film.

DUPLAY. ...Suzanne?

LOCKWOOD. That's right.

DUPLAY. Suzanne Crevel.

LOCKWOOD. That's her. She plays that part in the film. She's quite good, too. I mean, it's a cameo, but...

MIRIAM. Her sister's not in the film?

LOCKWOOD. Mademoiselle Cottard, I think that settles that. It's obvious I never met your sister. As for the letters…Frankly, I've no idea. Someone's idea of a joke, perhaps – a very sick joke.

JULIET. That's not true.

MIRIAM. Well, then, would you mind telling us what *is*? *(Pause.)*

DUPLAY. I thought you fired Crevel.

LOCKWOOD. What?

DUPLAY. You had a problem with her. We spoke about it when I visited you on location. She could not remember her lines…Something like that. Some sort of problem.

LOCKWOOD. With Suzanne? No.

DUPLAY. Now I remember. It was the first girl you fired. The one who…

(Silence.)

JULIET. I wonder what is true now, Monsieur Lockwood.

EMMA. So you never met the girl. Do you still expect us to believe that, Henry? *(Pause.)*

LOCKWOOD. Emma – what is it you want me to say?

EMMA. All I want you to tell me is what really happened. *(Pause.)*

DUPLAY. I think it is clear without a doubt that –

EMMA. I'd rather hear what Mr. Lockwood has to say, Alain. *(Pause.)* Henry?

(Silence.)

LOCKWOOD. All she had to do was walk up to the table, set the drinks down, exchange a few words with Cary, that was it…She couldn't do it. Simply couldn't do it. Take four, take five, take six…Cary was perfectly kind to her – you know how charming he is, Emma – I tried to get her to relax, I told her jokes…But in the end, I had to do it. I told Herbie we'd have to find someone else. And quickly. Time never more strongly resembles money than on a film set. You simply can't wait around for a bit player to get it right...Suzanne did it as a favor. One take, and we had it. We were still on schedule. *(Pause.)* That's the sum total of my experience with and knowledge of Liliane Bernard.

EMMA. ...And the letters?

LOCKWOOD. I only wrote that one.

JULIET. As far as you remember.

LOCKWOOD. It's the God's truth.

EMMA. Why did you write to her, Henry?

LOCKWOOD. ...Because she wrote to me. Several days after I'd dismissed her, I received a letter from her. Why had I fired her? Could she have another chance? Was I angry with her? Did I think she had any talent? Would she have a career? And so on and so forth. It all struck me as a bit – intense, given the circumstances. I mean, actors are hired and fired every day...But she was young. And intensity is youth's prerogative, isn't it?... So I wrote her back, trying to be as kind and as reassuring as I could be. I'm not out to destroy anyone's dreams, you know. I'm far too busy trying to realize my own.

MIRIAM. 'My fault entirely...You are not to be blamed for what happened.' ...It makes sense now. All it refers to is her being fired.

LOCKWOOD. And to nothing else whatsoever, I assure you.

JULIET. So you say.

EMMA. Can you offer a more plausible explanation, Mademoiselle?

JULIET. What he says is very reasonable. It seems there is an explanation for everything. Only one thing has yet to be explained: My sister is dead, Madame. Someone murdered her. Explain that, and I will accept anything you say.

DUPLAY. That is a matter for the Police, Mademoiselle.

JULIET. Shall I go to them now? Tell them all about this, and see what they say? *(Pause.)* Monsieur Lockwood? Is that what you wish me to do?

LOCKWOOD. ...There's no need for the Police.

JULIET. I didn't think you would want that.

EMMA. I disagree, Henry. Let's call this young woman's bluff.

DUPLAY. Madame Lockwood is right. These lies must be exposed. The facts must be made clear to the world.

LOCKWOOD. There's no need for the Police, Emma.

JULIET. Monsieur Lockwood is right. They will not take what he says without a question. *They* have nothing to lose – unlike your friends.

EMMA. Why don't you want the Police, Henry?

LOCKWOOD. Emma, I...You *know* how I feel about them.

MIRIAM. Mr. Lockwood, perhaps it's not a such a bad idea.

DUPLAY. Unfortunately, if one brings in the Police, one also brings in the newspapers. But let them come – there is nothing here to hide. I know that. And I know how to deal with the press.

LOCKWOOD. God, no. Not the papers. I don't want any of this – this...I don't want a word of what's been said in this room to go beyond these walls.

EMMA. You may not have a choice in the matter.

LOCKWOOD. I can't have that. I...No. I couldn't...I...

JULIET. I understand perfectly the attitude of Monsieur Lockwood. He knows very well that the Police will read the letters and the note and put the true story together. How one night, in this very hotel, a man – a famous man – took advantage of someone who was not famous and how, to keep his reputation and his money and his privilege safe, he –

LOCKWOOD. I won't listen to this!

JULIET. Would you like to hit me again, Monsieur Lockwood? Would that make it easier for you?

(She takes a pack of cigarettes and a lighter out of a jacket pocket.)

MIRIAM. What you've said isn't true.

JULIET. It is ugly sometimes, the truth.

DUPLAY. A lie is uglier, Mademoiselle.

JULIET. You should know, Monsieur, if you are a friend of his.

(*She lights her cigarette, exhales smoke.*)

Lying swine, all of you...Yes, maybe I will go to the Police.

MIRIAM. I think that's a splendid idea.

JULIET. *Comment?*

MIRIAM. I'll call the front desk right now. We could have them here in five minutes. – Mrs. Lockwood? May I call them?

LOCKWOOD. Miriam – please. No.

EMMA. Why do you want to bring them in, Miriam?

MIRIAM. Because, Mrs. Lockwood, sometimes the truth is even uglier than a lie.

DUPLAY. Miriam, what are you driving at?

MIRIAM. If we believe Mademoiselle Cottard...If we believe that Mr. Lockwood raped and then murdered this young woman's sister when she tried to blackmail him, the world would be a safer place with a raving lunatic like that behind bars...Am I right?...Mademoiselle Cottard? Don't you agree?

JULIET. ...Yes.

MIRIAM. If we believe that Mr. Lockwood is guilty of two such heinous crimes, the Police should immediately be informed of all the facts, an investigation should be undertaken, and Mr. Lockwood should be tossed in jail and the key should be thrown away.

EMMA. What's gotten into you, Miriam?

MIRIAM. Neither fame nor wealth nor privilege should protect such a monster from the law. Agreed?

LOCKWOOD. I thought you believed me, Miriam.

MIRIAM. Oh, I do, Mr. Lockwood. I'm simply saying what

should happen if Mademoiselle Cottard's story is true.

LOCKWOOD. You know it's not.

MIRIAM. I think I do.

DUPLAY. What is it, Miriam? Do you know something?

EMMA. For God's sake, Miriam, tell us what you mean.

(**MIRIAM** *picks up* **JULIET'S** *cigarette pack.*)

MIRIAM. May I have one of these?

JULIET. Certainly.

MIRIAM. Thank you.

(*She takes a cigarette from the pack.*

She picks up **JULIET'S** *lighter, lights the cigarette.*)

Merci.

JULIET. *De rien.*

MIRIAM. This is the same lighter Liliane Bernard used last night. How do you come to have it?

JULIET. I…I am afraid I…I do not understand.

MIRIAM. Oh, I'm sure there's a very simple explanation. I can think of several, actually. You each bought the same lighter from the same shop. Or she knew that you admired her lighter and she bought you one just like it. As a birthday gift, say. Those are possible explanations…I suppose.

(**JULIET** *rises.*)

Where are you going? To the Police? I'll call them and save you the trouble.

JULIET. I would like to have my lighter back, Madame.

MIRIAM. Yes, I'm sure you would. But for the moment, why don't you just sit down and shut up?

(*Pause.* **JULIET** *sits.*)

As I see it, there are two possibilities. Either your sister bought you this lighter or she gave it to you…That's the first option. The second option is this: your sister didn't buy you this lighter, she didn't give it to you, for the simple reason that you have no sister. That you are, in fact, Liliane Bernard. In which case...Well, you'll be lucky if the Lockwoods don't do everything in their power to tear you to bits.

LOCKWOOD. I'll wring her bloody neck!

EMMA. Henry! *(Pause.)*

MIRIAM. Well, Mademoiselle Cottard, which shall it be? Or should I say, which shall it be...Liliane?

(Silence.)

JULIET. There is a third option which you seem to have forgotten, Madame Stockton.

MIRIAM. Really? And what would that be?

JULIET. Has it occurred to you that – merely by chance – my sister and I have used the same brand of lighter?

MIRIAM. It has.

JULIET. But you insist that we are one and the same person?

MIRIAM. I do. *(Pause.)*

(Juliet opens her purse, removes items, places them on the coffee table.)

JULIET. My *carte d'identité*...A check for my salary this week...A letter from my lawyer concerning a rental property...and a *carte postale* from my father in Rheims. Look at them, Madame. They are proof that I am Juliet Cottard.

MIRIAM. I'm not interested in looking at forgeries.

*(**JULIET** turns to **DUPLAY**.)*

JULIET. Monsieur, would you look at these, please?

DUPLAY. Mr. Lockwood?

LOCKWOOD. Go ahead, Alain.

*(**DUPLAY** crosses to Juliet, takes the items.)*

JULIET. Monsieur, you will know a French document when you see one. Do these look like forgeries to you? *(Pause.)*

ALAIN. I am no expert, of course, but...as far as I can tell...

these are genuine.

EMMA. You're sure?

DUPLAY. I am afraid so, Madame. I would like nothing better than to say they are false, but...I see no reason at all to doubt them.

MIRIAM. ...They're not forgeries?

DUPLAY. No, Miriam...I'm sorry.

(He gives **JULIET** *the items.)*

JULIET. I will be happy to go and get my passport, Madame, if that would satisfy you. Then you may take it and the *carte* to the Police should you have any remaining doubts...It was the Police, was it not, you so very much wanted me to see? *(Pause.)* You are very smart. Too smart, I think. You needlessly complicate something that is very simple. Like Monsieur Lockwood and his movies...And tell me this: Even if this was the same lighter you saw last night, that I am indeed Liliane Bernard – and I am not, I swear to you – how could you prove it?

MIRIAM. I couldn't.

(Silence.

JULIET *puts the documents into her purse.)*

MIRIAM. ...I was so sure.

(Silence.)

EMMA. ...**MIRIAM,** I'd like to retire for the evening.

MIRIAM. Of course, Mrs. Lockwood.

(She helps **EMMA** *to her feet, escorts her out of the room.*

Silence.

MIRIAM *enters.)*

Mr. Lockwood?

LOCKWOOD. Yes?

MIRIAM. Mrs. Lockwood would like to see you.

LOCKWOOD. Tell her I'll be right in.

*(***MIRIAM** *exits.*

LOCKWOOD *rises.)*

I'll be back in a moment, Alain.

DUPLAY. Very good, Monsieur Lockwood.

*(***LOCKWOOD*** exits. Pause.)*

DUPLAY. ...*Ca va?*

JULIET. *Ca va...Et toi?*

DUPLAY. *Tout va bien.*

(Pause. Miriam enters.)

MIRIAM. ...Mademoiselle Cottard, this is rather difficult for me to say, but I must ask you to forgive me. I've only added to your burdens, and I feel horrid about it.

JULIET. I forgive you.

MIRIAM. I wonder – would it be terribly strange if I were to pour each of us a glass of wine? I think we could all use a drink at this point. Would that be horrible of me...given the circumstances?

DUPLAY. I see nothing wrong with that.

JULIET. I would appreciate it.

MIRIAM. Well, then...

(She rises, crosses to the drinks table.)

I don't expect any of us to become bosom companions, but we must try to keep things as civilized as we can.

DUPLAY. It is very gracious of you.

MIRIAM. Well, it'd all fall down around our heads otherwise, wouldn't it? The world...Alain, if you'd give this to Mademoiselle Cottard.

*(***DUPLAY*** crosses to ***MIRIAM***, *takes the glass, crosses to* ***JULIET***.*)*

DUPLAY. Mademoiselle.

JULIET. *Merci.*

*(***MIRIAM***, *with two glasses, crosses to* ***DUPLAY***.*

She gives him a glass.)

DUPLAY. *Merci,* Miriam.

MIRIAM. You're quite welcome.

(They sit.

LOCKWOOD *appears in connecting doorway.)*

MIRIAM. I have a sister myself, you know. In Portland. Portland, Oregon.

JULIET. I have heard of it, Madame.

MIRIAM. I know I'd be devastated if anything were to happen to her. We talk every day when I'm in Los Angeles. I can't imagine not seeing her or hearing from her. It'd break my heart.

JULIET. It has been...painful.

MIRIAM. You honestly mean to say that you hadn't seen or heard from your poor sister in...

JULIET. Almost a year from that day to this.

DUPLAY. How awful for you.

JULIET. Yes.

MIRIAM. No cards? Not even a letter? – I mean, apart from the note you received today?...Not even a telephone call?

JULIET. We were...not on good terms since...As I say, almost a year now. And now it is too late...

MIRIAM. So she never told you about – Mr. Lockwood and...

JULIET. The first I know of this is from her note with the letters.

DUPLAY. What a shock that must have been.

JULIET. Yes.

MIRIAM. You and your sister had no contact on any subject, in any fashion, in all that time?

JULIET. Not a word.

MIRIAM. And yet somehow you knew that the alleged assault supposedly took place in this hotel. How did you know that? *(Pause.)* Your sister couldn't have told you. By your own admission you hadn't spoken to her in months. In fact she swore to me that she'd told no one – no one at all. Neither Mr. Lockwood's letter nor the note make any reference to where the incident is supposed to have happened. And yet you spoke of its location with such force and conviction. How is that?

JULIET. What I said – what I said was...

MIRIAM. '*This – very – hotel.*' That's what you said. Those were your exact words. How could you have known that?...And please don't say, 'by telepathy.' I've had quite enough of Liliane Bernard and her eerie premonitions, thank you very much...There's no way you could have known what your sister said last night... Unless you – and she – are one and the same. *(Pause.)* The game's up, Liliane. It's time to go home.

(She tosses the lighter to **JULIET**.*)*

Thanks for the light.

(Silence.)

JULIET. ...I said no one would believe me. And I was right.

(She rises.)

It did happen. In this hotel. It happened.

LOCKWOOD. It couldn't have.

(They turn.)

We didn't stay here last October. Mrs. Lockwood wanted a change, said she was tired of this old place. So we stayed at the Ritz. *(Pause.)* You promised this girl some money in exchange for the letters?

MIRIAM. Five thousand francs. On the condition that she signed a statement protecting you from further... intrusions.

LOCKWOOD. Do you have the statement and the money with you?

MIRIAM. They're in my room. I'll go get them.

LOCKWOOD. If you would.

*(**MIRIAM** exits.*

Silence.)

...Is it true Casson turned you down?

DUPLAY. How did you know?

LOCKWOOD. Word gets around.

DUPLAY. I was afraid it would.

LOCKWOOD. Casson's an old friend of mine, you know.

DUPLAY. I didn't know that.

LOCKWOOD. We've been friends since the Silent days. I did rather a large favor for him once when he was running Gaumont. If you'd like, I'll have a word with him. He'll change his mind.

DUPLAY. Monsieur Lockwood, I...I am – overwhelmed.

LOCKWOOD. That's how it works, you know – one good turn deserves another.

DUPLAY. This is phenomenal. It's –

(*MIRIAM – manila envelope in hand – enters.*

She takes a folded letter from the manila envelope.)

MIRIAM. Mr. Lockwood.

(*DUPLAY crosses to LOCKWOOD.*

He embraces LOCKWOOD, kisses him on both cheeks.)

LOCKWOOD. That's quite...adequate, Alain. Thank you. I'm glad you're happy.

(*He moves out of DUPLAY'S embrace.*)

Miriam?

(*MIRIAM gives the letter to LOCKWOOD.*

He unfolds it, reads.)

You've covered all the bases. And the money?

MIRIAM. It's in here.

LOCKWOOD. Give it to me, please.

(*MIRIAM takes a smaller envelope out of the manila envelope, hands it to LOCKWOOD.*

LOCKWOOD crosses to the desk, picks up and uncaps a fountain pen.)

Mademoiselle?

(Pause. **JULIET** *crosses to the desk.)*

*(***LOCKWOOD** *holds out the pen.*

JULIET *takes it.)*

Your real name, if you don't mind.

(Pause. **JULIET** *signs.*

She sets the pen down.

LOCKWOOD *caps it, sets it aside.)*

The letters?

*(***JULIET** *takes a folded sheet of paper from her purse.)*

JULIET. There was only ever one.

(She places it on the desk.)

LOCKWOOD. And the note?

(Pause. **JULIET** *takes another sheet of paper from her purse.*

LOCKWOOD *picks it up.)*

…You have lovely handwriting, Mademoiselle.

(He sets the letter down.

He takes the money out of the envelope, thumbs through it.

He puts the envelope in a side pocket, then takes his wallet out of an interior breast pocket.

He takes a banknote from the wallet, drops it on the desk.)

There's a hundred francs…For your time.

(Pause. **JULIET** *picks up the banknote, puts it in her purse.)*

And you'll want your gun back, won't you?

(He takes out the key, unlocks the desk drawer.

He replaces the bullets, holds the gun out to her.)

Please. Take it. *(Pause.)* Don't worry. The safety's on. It won't go *boom.*

(Pause. **JULIET** *takes the gun, puts it in her purse.*
She crosses slowly to the door.)

JULIET. You and I, Monsieur Lockwood, we know the truth.

(Pause. She starts to exit.)

MIRIAM. Liliane.

*(***JULIET*** stops. Pause.)*

MIRIAM. You said something last night about a baby.

JULIET. Oh, there is a baby. But it's not Monsieur Lockwood's.

(Pause. She exits.
Silence.)

DUPLAY. She's a better actress than you thought.

*(***LOCKWOOD*** crosses to ***MIRIAM.****)*

LOCKWOOD. Here you are, Miriam.

MIRIAM. Thank you, Mr. Lockwood.

(She puts the smaller envelope inside the manila envelope.)

LOCKWOOD. Wherever did you get 5,000 francs?

MIRIAM. I cabled my mother in New York last night.

LOCKWOOD. Not your sister?

MIRIAM. Mr. Lockwood, I don't have a sister.

LOCKWOOD. …Miriam, my dear, you are what my mother would have called a pip. You must never leave us. Do you understand?

MIRIAM. Perfectly, Mr. Lockwood.

(He kisses her hand.)

And as for this young man…We're going to see that his film gets made. What do you think about that?

MIRIAM. That's smashing news. I'm so happy to hear it!

LOCKWOOD. Now, Alain, you've got to do something for me.

DUPLAY. Anything, Monsieur Lockwood.

LOCKWOOD. I want you to take this remarkable creature

down to the bar and buy her the biggest bottle of champagne you can find.

DUPLAY. It will be a pleasure, Monsieur Lockwood.

MIRIAM. Mr. Lockwood, that's so…so…

LOCKWOOD. Yes?

MIRIAM. Extravagant.

LOCKWOOD. It's been an extravagant evening. Why stop now?

MIRIAM. Well…All right. Yes. Why not? Why the bloody hell not?

LOCKWOOD. That's the spirit!

DUPLAY. Bravo, Miriam!

MIRIAM. Plus – we could stop at the front desk and put all this money in the hotel safe.

LOCKWOOD. You think of everything, don't you?

MIRIAM. I think my mother would hate to see her money go missing. I'd never hear the end of it.

DUPLAY. Madame Stockton?

(He takes her arm.)

MIRIAM. You'll join us, won't you? Oh, do say you will! Be extravagant!

LOCKWOOD. I'll tell you what. You run along, I'll look in again on Mrs. Lockwood, and then I'll join you in the bar. How does that sound?

MIRIAM. Like absolute bliss.

*(**MIRIAM** and **DUPLAY** start for the door.)*

DUPLAY. Hail the conquering heroine!

(They exit.

Silence.

LOCKWOOD *crosses to* **EMMA'S** *door, opens it slightly, looks in.*

He crosses to the sofa.

He removes and neatly folds his jacket, places it on the

sofa.

He crosses to the center of the room.

He kneels.

He folds his hands.

He lowers his head...

He crosses himself.

He rises.

He retrieves his coat, unfolds it, puts it on.

He walks over to the drinks table, pours himself a stiff glass of scotch.

He crosses to the couch, sits.

He sips his drink.

He begins to laugh...

Under his laughter a police siren is heard in the distance.

The siren grows louder...louder...

He rises, crosses to the balcony, steps out.

The siren cuts off.

MIRIAM *enters.*)

LOCKWOOD. Miriam, what is it? – What's happened?

MIRIAM. Liliane...

LOCKWOOD. What?…Miriam – what?

MIRIAM. …She's dead.

LOCKWOOD. How? What happened?

MIRIAM. We were…We were going toward the…the bar, and – she…she saw us, and came toward us, with the gun – it was aimed right at me. And Alain pushed me aside and threw himself at her, and…he tried to get it away from her, but it…it went off, and…He saved my life. She'd have shot me. She'd have...

LOCKWOOD. Oh, my poor, dear Miriam. My poor, dear girl.

MIRIAM. Alain told me to get my papers for the Police.

They'll ask all kinds of questions, he says, but he's going to handle it…He won't say anything, Mr. Lockwood. About this evening. He promised me he wouldn't.

(Pause. She crosses to the sofa, picks up Juliet's lighter.

She crosses to the desk.

She picks up the letter, sets it on fire, drops it into the waste paper basket.

LOCKWOOD *crosses to the desk.*

MIRIAM *picks up the note, sets it on fire, drops it into the waste paper basket.)*

Now no one will ever know.

LOCKWOOD. No one…but us.

(He sits behind the desk.

He begins to cry.)

MIRIAM. Oh, Mr. Lockwood, please don't…Please don't…

(She crosses to him, puts a hand on his shoulder.)

There…There now…

(Lights fade.)

2.

(Darkness.

Lights up.

Morning light through windows.

LOCKWOOD *on sofa.*

Whiskey bottle and glass on table.

EMMA *on balcony.)*

EMMA. It should be a beautiful day. *(Pause.)* We could take a cab to the Jardin Du Luxembourg...Or the Tuileries. That would be fine. Though I really prefer the Luxembourg. *(Pause.)* Miriam and Alain are going off to the Bois Du Bolougne, so there's no reason we have to stick around the hotel all day. *(Pause.)* Which would you prefer? The Tuileries or the Luxembourg?

*(***LOCKWOOD*** pours whiskey into his glass, drinks. Pause.)*

The Luxembourg it is, then.

(Pause. She crosses into the room.)

I think you're a damn fool behaving this way. I'd say you'd taken leave of your senses if you appeared to have any.

*(Pause. ***LOCKWOOD*** pours whiskey into his glass.)*

That's a marvelous solution, Henry. I recommend it highly. Drink until you pass out and finally get some sleep. Please. Don't let me stop you.

*(Pause. ***LOCKWOOD*** drinks.)*

God, sometimes you –

(Knock at door. Pause.

Another knock.

EMMA *crosses toward the door.)*

J'arrive...J'arrive.

(She exits. Pause.

She returns, letters in hand.)

Antoine had the morning post sent up.

(She crosses to the desk.)

Awfully nice of him. There'll be a large tip for Monsieur Antoine one of these next days...

(She sits, sorts through the mail.)

Well, well, well – let's see what we have here...A telegram from Darryl, wishing you all success and you still owe me a picture...Another telegram, and this is from... Oh, how nice!...It's from Jessie, bless her heart...You should see this one, it's very nice...Oh. this looks to be a letter from Grace and Rainier. From Austria, according to the postmark.

(She picks up the letter opener, slits the envelope, takes out the letter.)

I hope they're well...Seems they are...They're having a wonderful time in Vienna...They might be in Los Angeles this Fall...and they'd like very much to see us if they are. Well, I should very much like to see them. Such a handsome and charming couple...Do you remember the Christmas we spent with them? That was such a good time. Grace is so lovely but *so* wicked. She made me laugh so hard I thought I'd fall out my chair...I actually had to hold on to Rainier's arm so I wouldn't –

LOCKWOOD. Emma.

EMMA. Why, Henry Lockwood, as I live and breathe! What are you doing here?

LOCKWOOD. It's true. *(Pause.)*

EMMA. And this looks like a letter from Eric. You remember Eric? Claude's friend? They're both friends of Alain's, actually, they all work together on the –

LOCKWOOD. Emma. What she said. It's true.

(Pause. EMMA rises, crosses to LOCKWOOD. Pause.)

EMMA. Tell me.

LOCKWOOD. Not all of it's true, but…enough. *(Pause.)* Cary took a suite here when we came back from Nice. I arranged it with him. One night when you were out with Whit. *(Pause.)* Nothing happened, Emma. A lot of talk and a few kisses, that's all. I would have done more – I wanted to do more, but…

(He pours whiskey into his glass, drinks.)

I don't know why I did it. I wish to God I hadn't.

EMMA. So do I.

LOCKWOOD. When I think of how it's all turned out, of what…

EMMA. I know. *(Pause.)*

LOCKWOOD. I'll never do it again.

EMMA. Won't you? *(Pause.)* I know you, Henry. I've seen your films. I've even helped you write a number of them. I know you. Your mind is brimming over – is full to over-flowing – with lust and murder and hate…You long for what you can't have, and despise yourself for wanting it. You struggle desperately to control the appetites that torment you. You've built a cage for yourself out of work and habit and discipline. You feel trapped, you flail at the bars of your cage, but you know deep down that you need that cage. What animal would be unleashed if that cage didn't exist?…You're a weak man with an iron will. God forbid anyone should contradict you or prove you wrong. Your anger is as hot as your fear, and your fear is as deep as hell. Your desires are so forbidden, so loathsome to you, that you work like a slave to hide them – only to display them for all the world to see on a 40-foot screen…Chaos threatens with every step, but look how proudly you walk toward the abyss…While the pressure builds…And builds… So don't tell me it won't happen again. Don't tell me anything. I know you, Henry. As well as I know myself. Just because I hide behind my own mask doesn't mean I can't see behind yours. *(Pause.)* You're ashamed of yourself, aren't you?

LOCKWOOD. When haven't I been?

EMMA. Henry...

LOCKWOOD. You hate me, don't you?

EMMA. Sometimes. *(Pause.)*

LOCKWOOD. Do you want me to go?

EMMA. Go where?

LOCKWOOD. ...Away. *(Pause.)*

EMMA. Do you want to go away? *(Pause.)*

LOCKWOOD. No.

EMMA. Well, I don't want you to go away, either. *(Pause.)*

LOCKWOOD. But all those things...that you said...They're true.

EMMA. I was talking about your mind. But I also know what's in your heart. And what's there is so precious to me – so dear, so beautiful, so lovely and worthy of being loved – that not having that heart near mine would kill me. *(Pause.)* You're the only reason I cling to this wretched life, Henry. I'd die without you. *(Pause.)* I'm dying anyway, but...until then...I'm afraid – I'm afraid you're stuck with me. Just...Just don't ever put me through this again.

LOCKWOOD. I won't. Oh, Emma, I won't. I won't.

EMMA. I wish I could believe you.

LOCKWOOD. I wish you'd believe I'll try. *(Pause.)*

EMMA. You've had a long night, my darling. Go rest now.

*(Pause. **LOCKWOOD** rises, exits.*

Lights fade.)

3.

(Darkness.)

DUPLAY'S VOICE. Monsieur Lockwood, good morning.

LOCKWOOD'S VOICE. Good morning, Alain. Did you sleep well?

DUPLAY'S VOICE. I did, yes, thank you. So…Here we are again. What shall we talk about today? Shall we pick up where we left off?

(Lights up.

MIRIAM *– writing in notebook – at table.*

DUPLAY *– with pen and loose-leaf notebook – on sofa.)*

LOCKWOOD'S VOICE. That would be the logical thing to do, wouldn't it?

DUPLAY'S VOICE. Very much so, yes. We were talking about your work with writers.

LOCKWOOD'S VOICE. That's right.

DUPLAY'S VOICE. How do you feel about them?

LOCKWOOD'S VOICE. Writers, you mean?

DUPLAY'S VOICE. Yes.

LOCKWOOD'S VOICE. They're a necessary evil – but evil just the same.

*(***LOCKWOOD*** laughs.)*

DUPLAY. Miriam?

*(***MIRIAM*** hits the 'stop' button.)*

MIRIAM. Yes?

DUPLAY. I've finished looking at this part. I think it is very good.

(He rises, crosses to her.)

I have a few notes for you here. If you have trouble reading them, don't feel bad – my handwriting is a disgrace…Oh, and this part...

(He flips through the notebook.)

– right here. If you could check on these names. The spelling and so on...

MIRIAM. Certainly.

DUPLAY. And Monsieur Lockwood should look over the chapter on the silent films.

MIRIAM. I'll make sure he does.

DUPLAY. How is he, by the way?

MIRIAM. Sleeping like a log. Usually he's been up and about for hours by now, but the last few days have been hard on him.

DUPLAY. But he is all right?

MIRIAM. Oh, yes. There's nothing to worry about.

DUPLAY. And Madame Lockwood?

MIRIAM. She's having brunch with a friend downstairs.

DUPLAY. *Une femme extraordinaire.*

MIRIAM. Indeed.

DUPLAY. *Exactement comme toi, chere* Miriam. *(Pause.)*

MIRIAM. I do my best. *(Pause.)* You'd better be on your way. You don't want to be late.

(**DUPLAY** *glances at his watch.*)

DUPLAY. You are right – as always.

(*He crosses to the sofa, picks up a sheaf of papers.*)

MIRIAM. Are you excited?

DUPLAY. To meet with Casson?

MIRIAM. Yes. Are you nervous?

DUPLAY. Not at all…Well, perhaps a bit. But very much excited – yes.

(*He arranges the papers, puts them into his briefcase.*)

To think it could be this easy. All I do is sign my name, he signs his, and in one month – maybe two – we start filming. At last I make my movie.

MIRIAM. It must be a dream come true.

DUPLAY. I have been walking on the clouds from the moment he called.

MIRIAM. Well, before you float away completely, I'll take a quick look at your notes just to make sure I can read them…

(**DUPLAY** *closes his briefcase, puts on his white trench coat.*

He starts for the door, stops.)

...Ah. One more thing. Would you call Monsieur Bruhl in Liege and set up a screening of *Lost Virtue* for me?

MIRIAM. The Cinematheque doesn't have a copy?

DUPLAY. Damaged in the war.

MIRIAM. Oh...I'll call him today.

DUPLAY. You have the number?

MIRIAM. I do.

DUPLAY. *Superbe...*I should very much like to see it again. William Hayden, Anna Westerby, Derek Woolf, Raymond Fields in a small part...It's the best of the early sound films...You've seen it, of course.

MIRIAM. No, I haven't.

DUPLAY. My God, Miriam, you don't know what you have missed.

MIRIAM. What's it about?

DUPLAY. A man. A woman. A gun...It's fantastic.

(*He crosses back into the room, sets the briefcase down.*)

Guilt and voyeurism, the Flowers of Evil. All the themes are there, fully realized for the first time. And visually it is stunning. He took what he'd learned from the Germans and the Russians and made it his own...Also for the first time. In this film he is no longer merely working at a craft – he shows us he is a master. It is *breathtaking...*I can't believe you haven't seen it.

MIRIAM. Sad but true.

DUPLAY. Why don't you come with me? We'll see it together.

MIRIAM. Maybe.

DUPLAY. Liege is quite beautiful, Miriam.

MIRIAM. So I've heard.

DUPLAY. You would have a wonderful time.

MIRIAM. I'm sure I would.

DUPLAY. You must come. Say you will.

MIRIAM. Well, it's…it's awfully tempting, I admit.

DUPLAY. You know you want to.

MIRIAM. I'll think about it. *(Pause.)* There – I've thought about it.

DUPLAY. And what is your decision?

MIRIAM. I'll tell you this evening…Monsieur Director.

(He kisses her on the cheek.

As he starts to move away, MIRIAM *pulls him back and kisses him on the lips. Hard…*

They break.

DUPLAY *crosses to the door.)*

DUPLAY. *A bientot, ma chere.*

(He exits.

MIRIAM *opens the notebook.*

She leafs through it.

She stops.

She leafs back a few pages.

She stops.

She rises and – notebook in hand – crosses to the balcony windows.

She holds the notebook in the light from the window…

She closes the notebook.

She crosses to the couch.

She sits.)

MIRIAM. …No…No…

(She rises.

She crosses to the desk.

She opens a newspaper, flips through it.

She opens another newspaper, flips through it…

She picks up the desk telephone, dials.)

...Antoine? This is Miss Stockton in 225. Fine, thank you. Would you place a call for me?

...The Quai Des Orfevres...I'll hold...*Bon jour, Monsieur. Inspecteur Passavant, s'il vous plait...Passavant, oui. Inspecteur Passavant...Vous etes sure? Absolutement sure?... Merci, Monsieur...*

(She hangs up.

...She lifts the receiver, dials.)

Antoine, this is Miss Stockton. I'm sorry to bother you, again, but – is there anyone named Henri who works at the hotel?...May I speak to him?...Oh...Oh. I see... Well, thank you, anyway...Yes...Thank you.

(She hangs up the telephone.

She sits.

Silence.

Sound of a door opening.)

DUPLAY. *(off)* Miriam? *C'est moi.*

*(**DUPLAY** enters.)*

I was halfway there when I realized I had left my script behind.

(He picks up his briefcase.)

I can't have my meeting without that script.

*(He crosses behind the desk to **MIRIAM**.)*

The truth is, I left it behind just so I could come back to do this.

(He leans down to kiss her.

MIRIAM *pulls away.)*

...Miriam? What is it? Is something wrong? *(Pause.)*

MIRIAM. I've been thinking, Alain.

DUPLAY. About Liege?

MIRIAM. No...An idea for a film. May I tell it to you?

DUPLAY. Right this moment?

MIRIAM. I think you'll be interested.

DUPLAY. I have no doubt. But I also have no time.

MIRIAM. It's a murder mystery.

DUPLAY. Tell me tonight.

> *(He kisses her ear, exits.)*

MIRIAM. It's about a famous movie director and a French film critic.

> *(DUPLAY enters.*
>
> *Silence.)*

MIRIAM. You know how it is – sometimes an idea just comes to you, and there's nothing you can do but follow it to the end.

> *(DUPLAY crosses to the desk, sits opposite Miriam.)*

DUPLAY. What is this idea?

MIRIAM. I wouldn't want you to be late for your meeting.

DUPLAY. I think I can spare a minute.

MIRIAM. I haven't worked it all out yet.

DUPLAY. Perhaps I could help you.

MIRIAM. You don't mind listening to it?

DUPLAY. Please. *(Pause.)*

MIRIAM. A famous director comes to Paris for the premiere of his latest movie. While he's there, a French critic is conducting a series of interviews with the director for a film magazine.

DUPLAY. I like it so far.

MIRIAM. One evening the director's secretary is alone in the hotel room, working away.

DUPLAY. Transcribing the interview tapes?

MIRIAM. Yes. The director's wife is asleep in the other room. Her health isn't good. She has a heart condition and has to take it easy.

DUPLAY. Where is the director?

MIRIAM. At the movie premiere with the critic.

DUPLAY. Ah.

MIRIAM. The secretary leaves for a moment to look for a particular set of notes. When she returns, she finds a girl in a red coat waiting for her. The girl's in a terrible state. Eventually the secretary calms her down and finds out why she's there. The girl says she was raped by the director during the making of the film. Poor, hungry, half out of her wits, she's come to ask him for help.

DUPLAY. Does she have proof of what she says?

MIRIAM. A letter from the director that seems to validate her story.

DUPLAY. Seems to? Is there any doubt?

MIRIAM. The secretary…God help her…The secretary believes it. *(Pause.)*

DUPLAY. Go on.

MIRIAM. She tells the girl to come back the next afternoon; the secretary intends to buy the incriminating material and destroy it. The director and his wife will be spared.

DUPLAY. But the young woman doesn't show up.

MIRIAM. But someone else does…

DUPLAY. The Police?

MIRIAM. The critic.

DUPLAY. I didn't see that coming.

MIRIAM. The critic reveals that the girl in the red coat visited him, too. He admires the director greatly and promises to help the secretary any way he can. Together they will save the director from exposure, and the director's wife from the kind of shock that could seriously endanger her life…Even kill her.

DUPLAY. Very gallant, this critic.

MIRIAM. Yes, he is. He's also very, very…handsome.

DUPLAY. Does she have feelings for him?

MIRIAM. Yes. And she believes that he has feelings for her. They've been on the edge of…something…ever since they met. This crisis brings them together. Unites them.

DUPLAY. A love angle. That's very good.

MIRIAM. I thought so. *(Pause.)* That evening, another young woman arrives. She says she's the sister of the girl in the red coat – whose body was found in the Seine earlier that day. She has the letters and a note from her sister explaining what the director did. She claims the director murdered her sister. The secretary and the critic try to prove that she's lying. And they do. They demolish her story – even her identity. The secretary proves that the two sisters are really the same person. The whole thing was a trick, a...a scam. The young woman leaves in disgrace.

DUPLAY. End of scene.

MIRIAM. Not quite. When the director knows he's in the clear, he shows his gratitude to the critic by promising to help the him get his movie made. The critic wants to direct a film, you see, but no one will help him make it.

DUPLAY. I see him as brilliant but misunderstood.

MIRIAM. Or a vain, difficult, scheming monster who'd do anything to further his career.

DUPLAY. That is a matter of opinion.

MIRIAM. There's no denying he's ambitious.

DUPLAY. Or charming. *(Pause.)* Then what happens?

MIRIAM. The secretary and the critic go to the hotel bar for a bottle of champagne provided by the director. But just as they reach the lobby, the young woman steps into their path with a gun. She's going to kill the secretary –

DUPLAY. Or the critic.

MIRIAM. Or both...The critic and the girl fight for possession of the gun. The gun goes off accidentally – and the girl dies in the lobby. *(Pause.)* The critic deals with the Police. The secretary goes back to the director's hotel room and burns the note and Lockwood's letter.

DUPLAY. And *that's* the end of the scene.

MIRIAM. But not the end of the story. *(Pause.)* After everything's been cleared up, the critic brings along the bottle of champagne to the secretary's room. They go over the events of the past two days. At some point the secretary begins to cry.

DUPLAY. I can see it. He puts a gentle hand on her shoulder, he moves closer to her on the bed, soon he's kissing away her tears...

MIRIAM. She's laughing and crying, his body is so close to hers, his breath is so warm on her skin...

DUPLAY. Her smooth, soft skin...

MIRIAM. His strong, lithe body...

DUPLAY. They make love.

MIRIAM. They make love. *(Pause.)* When she wakes up next morning, he's there beside her. She watches him sleep. She watches him breathe. She can't believed what's happened to her. Everything – *everything* – has changed. Everything's transformed. The world's been made anew. *(Pause.)*

DUPLAY. For him as well.

MIRIAM. Really? *(Pause.)* The secretary carries with her wherever she goes her knowledge of the changed world. Her great secret, apparent to one and all. She's never been this happy, never this – blessed...But then...

DUPLAY. Yes?

MIRIAM. She's looking through the transcripts of the critic's interview with the director. And her heart freezes. *(Pause.)* She's wrong. She must be. She *has* to be. *(Pause.)*

DUPLAY. What is it about the transcripts?

MIRIAM. The critic's handwriting and the handwriting in the note – the note the young woman said came from her sister – are one and the same. The critic wrote the note.

DUPLAY. Is she sure about this?

MIRIAM. There's not a doubt in her mind...not after she checks the newspapers.

DUPLAY. ...I don't understand.

MIRIAM. She looks through the day's paper, and the paper for the day before, and there's not a single mention of a body pulled out of the Seine. *(Pause.)*

DUPLAY. Perhaps the news was suppressed to spare the family. Perhaps the family suppressed it themselves. There could be a dozen reasons why there is nothing.

MIRIAM. There could be. But the secretary doesn't stop there. She has to know.

DUPLAY. What does she do?

MIRIAM. Well – if there's no body, why did the Police tell the critic there *was*? The secretary calls the Police. She asks for the inspector the critic spoke to. But –

DUPLAY. There is no inspector by that name.

MIRIAM. That's right.

DUPLAY. ...So to whom did the critic speak?

MIRIAM. Whoever was at the front desk at the time. And who *was* at the front desk when the critic called? It wasn't the regular desk clerk. It was someone else. Someone the critic referred to as Henri.

DUPLAY. The critic arranged to have the regular desk clerk called away, and this Henri took his place.

MIRIAM. That's right. And what does the secretary do then?

DUPLAY. She...She calls the front desk and speaks with the regular desk clerk.

MIRIAM. And she asks about Henri.

DUPLAY. But the desk clerk tells her Henri did not come into work today.

MIRIAM. So where is he?...No one knows. Did he get drunk and thrown in jail?

DUPLAY. He might have quit his job...His wife might be ill...

MIRIAM. You're forgetting something – he'd know about the girl's death in the lobby. What if he put two and two together and started thinking that it wasn't accidental?

DUPLAY. That he was the only connection between the critic and his scheme?

MIRIAM. That he might be next…So he disappears.

DUPLAY. Or – and I admit this is extreme – he fell onto the Metro tracks on his way to work that morning and was crushed to death. It looks like an accident, but –

MIRIAM. The critic pushed him.

DUPLAY. And Henri's mouth is permanently closed. *(Pause.)* I like that. *(Pause.)* What happens next?

MIRIAM. That's all I've got. I was hoping you might have some ideas. *(Pause.)*

DUPLAY. This secretary is very clever, Miriam. Very clever. She builds a fascinating case against the critic. The problem is, it's only a theory.

MIRIAM. But a good one.

DUPLAY. With no proof, no evidence, there is nothing she can do. The critic cannot be touched. She can tell her story – but who will believe it? And what if they do? The critic has no reputation left to destroy. What does it matter if a few more people hate him? If the director and his wife despise him? If the secretary's heart is broken? He got what he wanted. He gets to make his movie. He will have won.

MIRIAM. But here's the thing, Alain. She *has* proof. *(Pause.)*

DUPLAY. She has? *(Pause.)*

MIRIAM. The note. *(Pause.)*

DUPLAY. She burned it.

MIRIAM. No, she didn't. She only *said* she did. The note is actually somewhere safe and sound and ready to be used whenever the secretary wishes…She tells this to the critic.

DUPLAY. Who does not believe her.

MIRIAM. Who would be foolish *not* to believe her. *(Pause.)*

DUPLAY. The critic would say something like, 'Prove to me that you have it. Show it to me.'

MIRIAM. And the secretary would say something like, 'What kind of idiot do you take me for?' *(Pause.)*

DUPLAY. She's bluffing. She doesn't really have the note.

MIRIAM. Oh, she has it. Her only question is what to do with it – and when. *(Pause.)*

DUPLAY. What does the secretary want from the critic?

MIRIAM. What do you think she wants?

DUPLAY. …Money?

MIRIAM. Say 50,000 francs?

DUPLAY. You could say that.

MIRIAM. Or a 100,000. That's even better.

DUPLAY. But the critic is poor. He couldn't pay that.

MIRIAM. He'd have to…Or go to jail.

DUPLAY. Would a 100,000 francs buy the note from the secretary?

MIRIAM. It might. If it was money she was after.

DUPLAY. Isn't it?

MIRIAM. What if it isn't?

DUPLAY. What else could it be?

MIRIAM. What do you think it could be?

DUPLAY. I…I don't know.

MIRIAM. Think! What else could she want?

DUPLAY. …Love?

MIRIAM. From the critic?

DUPLAY. Yes.

MIRIAM. That died when she recognized his handwriting and glimpsed the truth.

DUPLAY. So she wants revenge.

MIRIAM. Does she?

DUPLAY. *I don't know!*

(Silence.)

The critic would never stand for the situation. It would be *intolerable* to him.

MIRIAM. But what choice would he have? He's powerless. He'll never know a moment's rest. Never know when everything around him might collapse. It could happen this week…Or a year from now…Or in the next twenty minutes – just as he's about to sign the contract to make his first movie *(Pause.)* He'd have no choice but to accept it. There's nothing he can do. *(Pause.)*

DUPLAY. Miriam – what does she want?

MIRIAM. What do you think she wants?

DUPLAY. I want you to tell me.

MIRIAM. And I'm telling you to keep guessing.

DUPLAY. What does the critic do?

MIRIAM. You're a critic. What would *you* do?

(Silence.)

So – is this something you'd be interested in working on?

DUPLAY. No, I don't think so. Too implausible.

MIRIAM. Perhaps Mr. Lockwood would be interested in it. Or Casson.

(Pause. **DUPLAY** *laughs.)*

DUPLAY. Miriam, you are brilliant. Absolutely brilliant. You have created a story that I could never have imagined. *Felicitations.*

(He rises.)

…And goodbye.

(He starts for the door.

MIRIAM *rises.)*

MIRIAM. Where are you going?

DUPLAY. What it does matter when there is no place – no place at all – to go?…*Au revoir, chere* Miriam.

(He holds out his hand. Pause.)

MIRIAM. *Au revoir,* Alain.

(She takes his hand.

He pulls her toward him, spins her around, gets a fore-arm around her throat.)

DUPLAY. I want that note, Miriam. Give me the note, and I'll let you go.

MIRIAM. I…I don't have it.

DUPLAY. I don't believe you.

MIRIAM. Alain, please, listen to –

DUPLAY. Where is it?

MIRIAM. Alain, I…I –

(He tightens his grip.)

DUPLAY. Where is it?

MIRIAM. It's – it's in the…the desk. It's in the desk. It's in the desk.

DUPLAY. It had better be…Slowly, now…

(Keeping his grip around her throat, he maneuvers her over to the desk.)

Which drawer?

MIRIAM. Top – right.

DUPLAY. Open it.

MIRIAM. I can't reach it. You'll have to – I can't reach it…

*(**DUPLAY** lets his grip slacken enough for **MIRIAM** to reach out to the drawer.*

*But she grabs hold of the letter opener instead, and jabs it into **DUPLAY'S** side.*

She breaks his grip and stumbles away from him.

She exits.

***DUPLAY** staggers to the connecting door, locks it.*

Sound of pounding on door to hallway.

DUPLAY. I locked it, Miriam. You can't get away.

*(Pause. **MIRIAM** – letter opener in hand – enters.*

***DUPLAY** moves toward her.*

***MIRIAM** counters.)*

MIRIAM. Let me get to that telephone, Alain, or I'll stab you again.

(**DUPLAY** *moves toward her.*

MIRIAM *counters.*)

DUPLAY. You're not going to ruin it, Miriam. I want that note.

MIRIAM. Ruin – what?

DUPLAY. My film!

(*He moves toward her.*

MIRIAM *counters.*)

DUPLAY. I've never wanted anything more in my life, Miriam. Never. And you're not going to stop me. I want that note.

(**DUPLAY** *moves toward her.*

MIRIAM *counters.*)

What gave me the only pleasure, the only solace I had as a boy in the slums of Montmartre?

(*He moves toward her.*

MIRIAM *counters.*)

What helped me survive four long years of hell under the Nazis?

(*He moves toward her.*

MIRIAM *counters.*)

What sustains me – what keeps me alive – to this day?

(*He moves toward her.*

MIRIAM *counters.*)

"Night Train To Munich."

(*He moves toward her.*

MIRIAM *counters.*)

"To Have And Have Not."

(*He moves toward her.*

MIRIAM *counters.)*

"Castle On The Hudson." "The Lady From Shanghai."
"Beat The Devil." "This Gun For Hire." "On Danger-
ous Ground." "The Lady In The Lake." "He Ran All
The Way." "Kiss of Death."

(He moves toward her.

MIRIAM *counters.*

DUPLAY *catches her.*

He forces the letter opener out of her hand.

His hands find her throat.

They struggle toward the desk.

He pushes her onto it.

The recorder's 'play' button is hit, we hear LOCKWOOD
laugh, then:)

LOCKWOOD'S VOICE. I'm afraid of writers, actually.

DUPLAY'S VOICE. Why do you think that is?

LOCKWOOD'S VOICE. It's just part of a larger scheme of
– fear. I don't think a day goes by that not I'm desperately afraid. For one reason or another.

DUPLAY'S VOICE. But you must have some idea of why it
should like that.

LOCKWOOD'S VOICE. I don't know – and I don't want to!

*(*LOCKWOOD *laughs.*

MIRIAM *shifts –* Duplay's *grip slips –* MIRIAM'S *arm
brushes against the volume control.*

LOCKWOOD'S *laugh fills the room as* MIRIAM *claws at*
DUPLAY'S *face – he steps back – she falls to her knees
and begins to crawl away.)*

DUPLAY'S VOICE. Why don't you want to know?

LOCKWOOD'S VOICE. Some things are better left in the
dark, Alain - where they belong.

*(*DUPLAY'S *hand touches a reel of recording tape.)*

You know, people say to me, 'Oh Mr. Lockwood, why

do awful things happen in your movies?'

(*DUPLAY unwinds tape, wraps it around his hands.*

MIRIAM runs onto the balcony.)

MIRIAM. Help! Someone help me!

LOCKWOOD'S VOICE. I ask them, 'Why do awful things happen in life?'

DUPLAY'S VOICE. And what do they say to that?

LOCKWOOD'S VOICE. Nothing. Shut's 'em right up.

(*DUPLAY laughs.*)

LOCKWOOD. *(off)* Miriam?

(*Tape strung between both fists, DUPLAY starts toward MIRIAM.*

Pounding on connecting door.)

Miriam! What's happening? Unlock this door! Miriam!

DUPLAY'S VOICE. That's very good.

LOCKWOOD'S VOICE. I thought so.

MIRIAM. Someone help me! Please! Please help me!

(*DUPLAY steps onto the balcony.*

Pounding on connecting door.)

LOCKWOOD. *(off)* Miriam! I can't get to you! Miriam! Miriam!

LOCKWOOD'S VOICE. They think I'm joking, you know. But I'm not. That's the benefit of having a well-known character - it allows you to get away with murder.

(*DUPLAY stalks MIRIAM on the balcony.*

Pounding on connecting door.)

DUPLAY'S VOICE. In a manner of speaking.

MIRIAM. Help me! Help!

LOCKWOOD'S VOICE. Naturally.

(*Pounding on connecting door.*)

LOCKWOOD. *(off)* Miriam!

LOCKWOOD'S VOICE. On screen is where I put all my darker feelings. In real life I wouldn't harm a fly. I couldn't. I'm too afraid of getting caught.

(DUPLAY *gets the tape around* MIRIAM'S *throat, moves behind her.*

Pounding on connecting door.)

LOCKWOOD. *(off)* Miriam!

LOCKWOOD'S VOICE. The public thinks of me only as a sort of genial ghoul, a master of the macabre, 'The Sultan of Suspense,' as Crowther once called me. Well, do you know my opinion of that?

LOCKWOOD. *(off)* MIRIAM!

(DUPLAY *and* MIRIAM *stumble from the balcony into the room.*)

LOCKWOOD'S VOICE. As long as they buy tickets, they're free to think whatever they like.

DUPLAY'S VOICE. You may have fooled the public, but you haven't fooled me. I know what you really are.

LOCKWOOD. *(off)* MIRIAM!

LOCKWOOD'S VOICE. …and what is that?

DUPLAY'S VOICE. An artist, Mounsieur Lockwood - the equal of any I could name. I truly believe this, and someday...someday the world will know this to be true.

(*The connecting door flies open and bangs against the wall.*

LOCKWOOD *enters.*

DUPLAY *wheels about.*

MIRIAM *tears herself out of his grip.*)

LOCKWOOD'S VOICE. …Thank you…Thank you.

LOCKWOOD. I heard it all, Alain. I heard everything…I know what you are.

(*Pause.* DUPLAY – *howling* – *throws himself at* LOCKWOOD.

They struggle.

DUPLAY *freezes.*

He grabs his chest…sinks to the floor.

LOCKWOOD *crosses to* **MIRIAM**, *helps her to the couch.)*

LOCKWOOD. Miriam. Are you all right? Tell me you're all right.

MIRIAM. Oh, Mr. Lockwood…He…He was…

LOCKWOOD. I know, Miriam, I heard it all.

EMMA. *(off)* Henry, I'm back!

*(**EMMA** enters, key in hand.*

She stops.)

What in the name of…

(She crosses to **DUPLAY**, *kneels, feels his pulse.)*

Henry, get my medicine. I think he's had a heart attack.

*(**LOCKWOOD** doesn't move.)*

Henry!

(He exits.)

MIRIAM. Is he dead?

EMMA. No. – A glass of water. Quickly.

*(**MIRIAM** crosses to the drinks table.*

EMMA *undoes* **DUPLAY'S** *tie and collar, gets a pillow from the sofa, places it under his head.*

LOCKWOOD *– with medicine bottle – enters.)*

LOCKWOOD. Is this it?

EMMA. Yes. – Bring me the water, Miriam.

*(**EMMA** takes the medicine from Lockwood.*

LOCKWOOD *slumps onto the couch as* **MIRIAM** *crosses to* **EMMA** *with a glass of water.*

EMMA *removes the bottle's stopper.)*

What in the name of God happened here tonight?

MIRIAM. He planned it all, Mrs. Lockwood. The blackmail, the visit from Juliet – all of it. He killed her. And he tried to kill me, too. And Mr. Lockwood.

EMMA. Henry, is this true?

LOCKWOOD. Yes, Emma. It's true.

EMMA. ...Alain did this to us?

(Pause. She replaces the bottle's stopper. Pause.)

Put this back in the medicine cabinet, Miriam.

MIRIAM. But, Mrs. Lockwood, he...He'll die if we don't help him.

EMMA. Yes, he will. *(Pause.)* He'll die, won't he, Henry?

LOCKWOOD. If we don't help him.

(Silence.

MIRIAM *takes the medicine bottle from* **EMMA**.*)*

MIRIAM. I'll put this back for you, Mrs. Lockwood.

EMMA. Thank you, Miriam.

*(***MIRIAM** *exits. Pause.)*

Call the front desk, Henry. Tell them we need an ambulance...And the Police.

(Pause. **LOCKWOOD** *rises, crosses to the telephone table, picks up the receiver.)*

...We were too late, that's all. Simply too late.

LOCKWOOD. What could we have done?

EMMA. Nothing. We were too late.

*(***LOCKWOOD** *dials.*

MIRIAM *enters.*

She crosses to **EMMA**, *who takes* **MIRIAM'S** *arm in hers.*

Lights begin to fade.)

LOCKWOOD. ...*Bon jour*, Antoine. This is Mr. Lockwood in 225. I'm afraid we've got a bit of an emergency here... Yes, I'm afraid so...Yes...

(Lights fade.

Darkness.)

PROPERTY PLOT

ACT I
Scene 1

Lockwood/Duplay: A reel-to-reel tape recorder with microphone.
Henry: A letter opener.
Emma: A cane and a book.
Henry/Emma/Duplay/Miriam: Liquor/wine bottles and glasses.
Miriam: 4 telegrams, several packages (one of which contains four or five books).
Duplay: A pack of French cigarettes.
Miriam: A small bottle of medicine, a bottle of Evian water and a glass.
Miriam: Several notebooks and fountain pen.

ACT I
Scene 2

Liliane: A leather briefcase with papers.
Miriam: a bottle of brandy and a glass.
Liliane: a pack of French cigarettes and a lighter.
Lilliane: A purse, an envelope with a letter inside.
Miriam: A pair of glasses.
Miriam: A purse with period paper French money.
Miriam/Emma: Wineglasses.
Miriam: A hand towel (to wipe up spilled wine).

ACT I
Scene 3

Miriam: A cigarette.

ACT I
Scene 4

Juliet Cottard: A pistol.

ACT II
Scene 1

Lockwood: Bullets (from Juliet's gun).
Juliet: A purse, a note, an envelope with a letter inside.
Juliet: A pack of French cigarettes, a lighter (the same lighter that Liliane used in Act I, Scene 2).
Juliet: A carte d'identite, a check, a letter, a carte postale.
Miriam: A manila envelope containing a folded letter and an envelope with French paper money.
Lockwood: A wallet with a 100-Franc note.
Lockwood: A whiskey bottle and glass.

ACT II
Scene 2

Lockwood: A whiskey bottle and glass.
Emma: Two telegrams and two or three letters.

ACT II
Scene 3

Miriam: A fountain pen and notebook.
Duplay: A fountain pen and loose-leaf notebook.
Duplay: A sheaf of papers, briefcase (same briefcase as in Act I, Scene 2).
Miriam: Two copies of a period French newspaper.
Duplay: A reel of recording tape.
Miriam/Emma: A glass of water, and the medicine bottle from Act I, Scene 1.

COSTUME PLOT

ACT I
Scene 1

Henry Lockwood—formal evening wear.
Alain Duplay—formal evening wear.
Emma Lockwood—dress.
Miriam Stockton—business wear: jacket, blouse, skirt, hat, gloves.

ACT I
Scene 2

Miriam—same outfit as before, minus jacket, hat and gloves.
Liliane Bernard—red coat over cheap dress.
Emma—silk dressing gown over silk robe.

ACT I
Scene 3

Miriam—another blouse and skirt.
Alain—white trench coat over a dark suit.
Henry—dark suit.
Emma—red coat over expensive dress.

ACT I
Scene 4

Miriam—the same.
Alain—the same, minus trench coat.
Henry—the same.
Emma—the same, minus red coat.
Juliet Cottard—gray suit; hat and gloves; spectacles.

ACT II
Scene 1

ALL—the same.

ACT II
Scene 2

Emma—another dress.
Henry—same outfit as before, minus jacket and tie.

ACT II
Scene 3

Miriam—another blouse and skirt.
Alain—white trench coat over dark suit.
Lockwood—dressing gown over shirt and trousers.
Emma—another expensive dress.

Also by
Joseph Goodrich...

Smoke and Mirrors

Please visit our website **samuelfrench.com** for complete
descriptions and licensing information